No Monsters in the Closet

No Monsters in the Closet

by Willo Davis Roberts

Aladdin Books
Macmillan Publishing Company
New York
Maxwell Macmillan Canada
Toronto
Maxwell Macmillan International
New York Oxford Singapore Sydney

Aladdin Books
Macmillan Publishing Company
866 Third Avenue
New York, NY 10022

Maxwell Macmillan Canada, Inc.
1200 Eglinton Avenue East
Suite 200
Don Mills, Ontario M3C 3N1

Macmillan Publishing Company is part of the Maxwell Communication
Group of Companies.
Printed in the United States of America
10 9 8 7 6 5 4 3 2 1

Library of Congress Cataloging-in-Publication Data
Roberts, Willo Davis.
    No monsters in the closet / Willo Davis Roberts. — 1st Aladdin
  Books ed.
      p.   cm.
    Summary: Steve's investigation of a haunted house that seems to be
  in use involves him with criminals who think he knows too much.
    ISBN 0-689-71577-3
    [1. Mystery and detective stories.]   I. Title.
  PZ7.R54465No   1992
  [Fic]—dc20   91-46059

No Monsters
in the Closet

1

My dad always said I had too much imagination for my own good. Only the day before it started he'd bawled me out because of the stories I'd been telling my little sister Cindy about the slimy purple creature that lived at the back of my closet. So nobody believed me when I remarked that maybe the old Hanson house was haunted.

I'll admit I made up the monster in the closet. I thought Cindy *liked* hearing my wild stories; when I asked her later, she said she *did*, except they made her have nightmares. After my mom and dad got pulled out of bed three nights in a row because Cindy was yelling, "No, no, don't eat me!" or something like that, Dad wanted to know what was going on.

"Listen, Steve," he said to me, "we have to be able to get some sleep around here. Cut it out with the horror stories."

So when I told them about the Hanson house, Dad gave me a threatening look. "Don't start that again, OK?"

I knew he meant that dirty look, so I shut up. But I wasn't making it up about the Hanson house. Something peculiar was going on there.

The Hanson house is about a block down from ours, on Maple Drive. It's a nice street, with mostly big, not very new, houses. The Hanson place is one of the older ones. It sits well back from the street and is shaded by big maple trees and some prickly kind of bushes that make a hedge on both sides from the street to the alley.

The Hanson house had been empty for ages. Dad said it was because it needed a lot of work done on it, before old Mr. Hanson's son could rent it out, and nobody wanted to pay for the work. Old Mr. Hanson had had a stroke or something and had to go to live with his son. Once in a while the son, Harold Hanson, came around to check things out. But mostly it just sat there.

I tried to keep track of who moved in and out

of the neighborhood because I peddled papers. In the morning I delivered the *Times,* and in the afternoon I delivered the *Herald.*

The newspapers were always having contests to get more customers. That's how I got my bike. I won a few smaller things, too, like free tickets to the movies and gift certificates for Rotten Ralphie's hamburgers. He makes the best hamburgers in town.

There was a contest on now, with a prize I really wanted, a radio-tape-player. My brother Mark and I had one in our room, only it was too big to carry around. This one was small enough to carry with me on my bike; I thought it would be great to have music to keep me company when I was riding around through the empty streets in the morning.

To win it, I needed to get some more customers. I wasn't a cinch to win, though I had a big route, because Shorty Bergen had a big *Times* route, too, and I knew he was working just as hard to win as I was.

That first day I noticed something odd at the Hanson place I wasn't delivering papers though. I was walking home from the show with the Swan twins. We'd been to see this movie about these aliens from outer space who came down and established a base for their spaceship near a swamp.

Ricky was being silly, lifting his arms and pretending to fly. "I hope they can *really* get a spaceship to some distant planet by the time I'm old enough to go along," he was saying, just as we were passing the empty house. And looking up, I caught a flicker of light back there in the trees.

"Hey." I stopped. "I saw something."

Ricky dove dramatically for the gutter, flattening himself on the pavement. "Get down, quick! Before they see us and take us into their ship!"

"Who?" Ray asked. "I don't see anybody."

"The aliens!" Ricky whispered. "I saw it, too, there's a light back there!"

"Well, it's not likely it's aliens," Ray said. "Probably some guy putting out his garbage or looking for his cat."

"Nobody lives there, stupid," Ricky reminded him.

"Maybe it's ghosts," I said lightly. "Do ghosts ever use flashlights?"

"No," Ricky said, getting out of the gutter. "They glow all by themselves."

Ray and Ricky look just alike. I can only tell which is which at close range. Ricky has the same blond hair and blue eyes, but there's something different with his teeth. He has a small space between the two front ones. So if he grins I know it's him. If he keeps his mouth shut—which he doesn't do very often—it's harder to tell.

I wasn't paying any attention to them. I was moving back along the sidewalk so I didn't have to look through the shrubbery. "I don't see anything now, but I'm sure there was a light."

Ricky came with me. "Maybe there's a fire."

"If there was a fire," Ray pointed out, "we'd still see it. Wouldn't we?"

"Let's go look, anyway," Ricky said. "There isn't supposed to be anybody around in there."

It was kind of spooky with all that untrimmed hedge on both sides. The house was two stories high, painted gray with white trim, though you couldn't really tell that at night.

"I don't see anything," Ray said, stopping at the bottom of the front steps.

I started around the corner of the house, following the sidewalk to the rear. The twins trailed behind me, Ricky making his usual remarks. "What if there's a spaceship back there, landed in that big back yard? We going to talk to them?"

He grunted when his brother hit him. About that time I reached the end of the sidewalk. There wasn't anything or anybody there, except a smell.

"Hamburgers," Ray said, mystified. "I smell hamburgers."

"Yeah, so do I," I agreed. "Rotten Ralphie's."

We didn't find any sign of invaders, or hamburgers, so we finally went on home.

But I was sure I'd really seen a light, maybe a flashlight, and I wondered who had been poking around and why.

I was curious enough so that the next afternoon, after I'd run my *Herald* route, I left my bike in front of the place and walked around the house again. I even tried the doors. Looking at it up close, I couldn't think why anybody would want to break in. Nobody'd lived there for several years, and it didn't seem that anything worth stealing remained.

The doors were all locked. The garage out behind the house was locked. I shrugged. Maybe I'd imagined seeing something.

That made me late for supper. But for once I wasn't the only one. Mom looked around from where she was dishing up carrots and broccoli and said, "Where's Cindy?"

"I don't know. I haven't seen her since breakfast."

Mom's worry lines showed up in her forehead. "Well, go look for her, will you, Steve? Maybe she met a friend and got delayed. And hurry. Your dad's got bowling tonight, remember? He's going to have to go ahead and eat."

It smelled good and I wouldn't have minded eating, myself, but I turned around and went to look for Cindy. She's only seven, and keeping track of the time isn't one of the things she does best.

I wasn't really worried about her. Nothing ever happens to kids in our neighborhood. Most likely she was squatting somewhere watching ants carry away crumbs, or with her foot stuck in a sewer grating or something. Those things had happened before.

She wasn't stuck, but a pup was. I found her half a block away, on her stomach beside a hole where somebody was fixing a pipe or something. She looked up when I yelled at her.

"Oh, Steve, I'm glad you're here! I can't get him out!"

"Who?" I asked, putting aside my bike. And then I saw.

"He fell in the hole," Cindy said unnecessarily. "I can almost reach him, but not quite. They shouldn't leave holes standing around like this."

I had to agree. I looked down at the pup, who barked piteously. He was so skinny I wondered how long he'd been there.

9

I got down and reached for him, hauling him out. He looked to be four months old or so, a sandy-colored dog with big feet and a big head, too. He licked gratefully at my ear.

"If the hole isn't filled in tomorrow," I said, "I'll ask Dad who to call about it. What do you think you're doing?"

Cindy had picked up the dog, leaving muddy smears on her shirt; he was now licking *her* ear.

"I'm going to keep him," she said.

"Cindy, Mom isn't going to let you keep him. Besides, he probably belongs to somebody."

"Does he look like he belongs to somebody?" she demanded. "He's starving, and he hasn't got a collar."

I threw up my hands. "All right. Come on, let's go, we're late for supper. You can argue with Mom about the dog."

Mom and Dad looked at the pup with the doubt I'd expected. "He looks like a Great Dane," Dad guessed. "If he grows up to those feet and that head, he's going to be a monster."

"Really?" Cindy asked excitedly.

"Not that kind of monster, Cindy. I meant he'll be a *big* dog. I don't think we want a dog, honey. We're all busy people. There's no one to look after him, train him."

"I'll help," Mark said.

"At least let's keep him for tonight," Cindy begged. "And feed him. He's hungry, Mom."

That was how we got Sandy, which is what Cindy called him. We tried to find his owner and couldn't, and by that time everybody was getting sort of attached to him.

It was Sandy who got me involved in what was going on over at the Hanson house.

2

A few days later, on my paper route in the morning I saw a power company truck in front of the Hanson place, and I stopped to wait until the meterman came back from the side of the house.

"Hi," I said.

He looked at me. "Hi."

"How come you're reading the meter?" I asked. "Somebody moving in?"

"Don't ask me," he said. "All I do is read the meter."

"Why read the meter if the electricity is turned off?" I wanted to know.

"Because I guess somebody wants it turned back on."

12

"Oh. Well, thanks." I watched him drive away. If they were going to turn the power back on, maybe I'd get another customer. I'd keep watch for signs people were moving in.

I met Shorty Bergen downtown that afternoon when I was getting a new pair of running shoes. I got black ones, with red slashes on the sides, and I was admiring the way they looked on my feet so I nearly ran into Shorty.

"Maybe you need glasses," Shorty said. "I know I'm not very big, but most people can see me. They don't step on me."

"Sorry. How many new customers have you got, for the new contest?"

"Fifteen," he said. "How many you got?"

"Twelve," I had to admit.

"I got two more customers lined up, I think," he added. "My uncle's going to subscribe, and my cousin that went in the army. We're going to mail his to him."

I wasn't sure that was fair, mailing copies.

"Well, good luck," I said insincerely, and heard him laugh when I walked past him. "Sure, good luck," he said, and I knew he didn't mean it any more than I had.

I walked half a block and paused to look in the window at Smitty's Video and Stereo Shop. I was a good customer of Smitty's, and he was one of mine. He took the *Herald,* and the *Times* just on Sundays because he liked their comics. When I could afford it, I bought tapes from Smitty.

There was a new one out that I wanted, by the Dogs in the Manger. Mom thinks their name is so awful their music couldn't be any good, but it is. Lots of drums and guitars, and a good bass. I like a lot of bass. I couldn't afford it now, though.

Cindy met me when I got home. "Steve, you have to help! Sandy's missing!"

"Maybe he went back where he came from," I suggested.

"No, he didn't! He likes it here! Dad said to keep him in the backyard, and I *did*, only Mark left the gate open, and Sandy got out. Help me look, Steve."

"I've got papers to deliver," I reminded her. "I'll keep an eye out for him on my route. Get Mark to help you, it's his fault the dog got away."

"He's already looking," Cindy said. "He hasn't found him yet." She looked as if she might cry, so I gave her a stick of gum and picked up my bag of papers.

Things went pretty smoothly on my route, but then as I came past the Hanson place, I saw a familiar figure trotting around toward the back of the house.

14

"Hey, Sandy, here, Sandy!" I yelled. The darned fool dog paused and looked at me, then kept on going.

I muttered something under my breath about what I was going to do to Mark when I got home, left the bike and the few remaining papers on the unmowed front lawn, and headed after Sandy.

He'd disappeared. I looked around, figuring he must have gone on through to the alley, maybe to investigate garbage cans. If he caused that kind of trouble, I wasn't sure how long he'd last around the Quentin house. My dad operates Quentin's Building Supply—that means lumber and hardware—and he prides himself on dealing fairly with everybody and not annoying his neighbors. That includes the rest of the family, too. I mean, we're not supposed to annoy anybody, either.

My guess was that Sandy was going to break that rule.

I went around behind the Hanson garage and looked down the alley. Sure enough, there he was, half a block away. When I called, he didn't pay any attention to me.

I wasn't going to leave my bike and papers to pursue some stupid pup down an alley, I decided, and started back to the street.

The driveway went from the alley through the

yard, where you could either drive up to the back door or turn into the garage. I stopped and looked at something I hadn't noticed when I checked the place out before.

There was a puddle of oil on the gravel that must have leaked out of someone's car very recently.

Not the meter reader, he'd parked on the street and walked in. Mr. Hanson drove a new Cadillac; I was sure *his* car didn't leak oil. By the time I got home, Sandy had decided he was hungry for something better than garbage and was eating out of his dish in the kitchen.

"He came home," Cindy announced happily.

"Keep the gate closed from now on," I said to Mark.

"Sure, I'll be more careful," Mark agreed.

Only *somebody* wasn't careful, because the next day Sandy got out again. This time he did more than prowl among the garbage cans in the alley. This time he stole something.

I was sprawled out on my bed, listening to a tape by the Rocking Rovers, and reading a new mystery, when I heard a "Psssst!"

"Steve! I need help!"

I sighed and put down the book. "What, Cindy? What've you done this time?"

"I haven't done anything. It's Sandy! Look what he brought home!"

I sat up, then, because she tiptoed into the room dangling something from a leather strap. She put it in my hand.

"A watch? A good man's watch? Where did he get it?"

"I don't know. It runs, it tells the right time. Why would a dog steal a watch?"

I wondered the same thing, but was already figuring it out. I lifted it close to my nose. "It smells like hamburgers, or roast beef or something." I sniffed again. "Yeah, see? It has something spilled on it, maybe juice off a hamburger."

"What shall we do? I never thought we'd have a dog that was a thief," Cindy said. "Where did he get it?"

I groaned. "How am I supposed to figure out where he got it? It could have come from anywhere within a couple of miles."

I got a clue, though, when Sandy ambled into the room a minute later. He wagged his tail and came to put an oversized paw onto my knee.

"Mom's going to be mad," Cindy said in hushed voice. "He made tracks on the kitchen floor."

"This is a wonderful dog you brought home," I told her.

I shoved his foot off my knee, then stared at the faint marks left on my faded old jeans. "Come back here. Lie down, Sandy, let me see your feet."

Mark and Cindy had both been working with him; and if he felt like it, he'd obey a few simple commands. I examined his front paws. There wasn't much left—he'd already tracked it on the kitchen floor—but when I spread the pads apart I could still see it.

Oil. Black, gooey motor oil. I bent over and smelled it to be certain.

I had dropped the stolen watch on my bed where it was right at eye level as I knelt beside the dog. The two things together, the oil on his feet and the watch strap that smelled of cooked meat, clicked in my mind.

"The Hanson house."

"What?"

"I've seen oil in the gravel and smelled hamburgers at the old Hanson place. Maybe that's where he got it."

Cindy's brown eyes were big and scared. "What'll we do? Will they send the police after him?"

"They don't very often arrest dogs," I assured her. "Only I guess I better try to return it." Annoyance rose inside me. "Who let him out this time?"

"I don't know. He just got out. Will you try to keep him from being punished for stealing the watch, Steve?"

I sighed. "I guess so. Only for crying out loud, find some way to keep him home, will you?"

I pulled the tape out of the tape deck and put a marker in my book. "I'll go over there and see what I can do."

It wasn't a job I looked forward to. I hoped the guy who owned the watch would be glad enough to get it back that he wouldn't be angry about it being stolen in the first place.

I put the watch in my pocket and went over there. The puddle of oil had seeped into the gravel a bit more, but there was still enough to come off on my finger when I touched it. It smelled just like what had been on Sandy's paw.

There was nobody around. The place was the same as it had been, deserted, abandoned, except for that oil that proved somebody had been there recently.

I cleared my throat and called out. "Anybody here?"

There was no answer. I felt sort of silly. The watch had come from somewhere, though, and if it hadn't been from here, I didn't have the slightest idea where else to look.

By this time I'd decided I didn't really care much for dogs, at least not until they were past the puppy stage.

I walked up on the porch to the back door. I could see through the uncurtained window, and the kitchen sure didn't appear to be occupied, though it had cabinets and a range and a refrigerator in it. The refrigerator looked a hundred years old.

I knocked on the door. What was I going to do if somebody came? Hand over the watch and run, or what?

It didn't matter. Nobody came. Now what? I wondered.

Then I smelled it again. Hamburgers. With onions.

Just like on the watch band.

This time I tried to find where the odor came from, and there it was. Greasy stains, mayonnaise or some of Rotten Ralphie's special sauce, smeared on the boards of the porch.

Would Sandy have left any traces of the sauce if he'd been the one to steal the watch?

He might have, if somebody'd chased him off before he finished what he was trying to do. I tried to figure it out. Maybe somebody had been working here, fixing some of the things that needed to be repaired, and they'd bought lunch at Rotten Ralphie's and made the mistake of setting the bag down on the porch. And along came a puppy who didn't know any better. He'd helped himself to whatever smelled good, including the watch with the sauce spilled on it.

Well, I didn't know how to hand the watch over to its owner if I couldn't find him. Maybe the best thing to do was just to leave the watch where the guy would find it if he came back.

Where, though? If I left it on the floor of the porch and Sandy escaped from our yard again, he might take it a second time. I'd better find a safer place than the porch to leave it.

I didn't think about it when I tried the door, that it had been locked before. But I remembered at once, when the knob turned and the door swung inward.

I saw then that someone *had* been in the house. There were two pop cans sitting on the counter, and a torn bag from Rotten Ralphie's.

The bag was torn. I pictured it, the guy trying to get a key in the lock while juggling the bag and maybe the pop cans, the bag rips and a hamburger falls out on the porch. Before the guy can retrieve it, Sandy pounces on it. That didn't tell me where the watch came in, but I was pretty sure by this time that the watch really did belong here.

I pulled it out of my pocket and laid it on the counter beside the empty bag. Then I went out, closed the door and went down the steps. I decided to go home through the alley, and I'd started that way when I realized there was something different about the house.

I stopped and looked at it carefully. What was it?

And then I saw. The basement windows across the back of the house had a blank look they hadn't had before. I vaguely remembered noticing that they were dirty, cobwebby actually. The cobwebs were still there, only now there was cardboard over the windows, on the inside.

Why would anybody do that? I wondered. Well, it was none of my business. I shrugged and walked away. It wasn't my problem.

For once I didn't try to use my imagination.

3

Saturday was my favorite day. I delivered the *Times* before anybody else was up, and then I had all day to do whatever I wanted to do until it was time to deliver the *Herald*. Partly what I liked to do was take a good book up to my room and sprawl on the bed and read while I listened to music. I like to eat, too, so I usually had a sandwich or two, a granola bar, and some fruit; it didn't seem too much to ask to be allowed to do these simple things in peace.

Getting any peace around our house is a really good trick.

Saturday was a big day at the Builder's Supply; all the do-it-yourselfers were out in force, Dad said, so he had to be on hand to explain to them how to fix their own roofs or change washers on their faucets or build doghouses or repair their porch steps. Most of the time he didn't even get lunch.

That meant if there was anything that needed doing around our house, *I* was asked to do it. So Mom stood in my bedroom doorway while I was trying to listen to the Bombay Bats with one ear, and keep half my mind on the book I was trying to read, while I listened to her list.

"Be sure to take out the garbage, Steve. You'd better finish pruning the apple tree, and get the branches out in the alley where they'll get picked up. My shoes are supposed to be resoled by today; would you pick them up when you finish the *Herald* route this afternoon? I'm going over to Aunt Lucille's this morning to help with the planning for Laurie's wedding, so fix something for Cindy for lunch, will you?"

My Saturday started being chopped to pieces before it was well started.

I got up and finished the apple tree. It was almost done, so it didn't take long. Then she was gone and I thought I ought to be able to read in peace until lunch. In the afternoon, I was going to the show with the Swan twins. I had fortified myself with a peanut butter sandwich, a can of Pepsi, and an apple, and was all settled in when Cindy appeared at the foot of my bed.

I looked up and saw the tears on her face and sighed.

"What's the matter?"

I could see she'd been crying. "I was taking Sandy for a walk. I had him tied on a string, but it broke."

I groaned. "Oh, no! Cindy, I can't spend my whole life looking for that fool dog! Where did you lose him?"

"I didn't lose him, exactly. I know where he is," Cindy said, leaning against the foot of the bed.

"Where?"

"I guess he remembered where he got the watch that smelled like hamburgers. He went back over there."

"And he won't come when you call him?"

"He can't," Cindy said. Two more tears spilled over.

"What do you mean, he can't?" I sat up, figuring however this came out, I wasn't going to be able to go on reading.

"He went in the garage, and he's locked in. I couldn't get him out."

"How could he get locked in?" I demanded. I was already reaching for my shoes.

"I don't know. He ran in there, I guess, and they shut the door. By the time I got there, the door was locked. I called him, and he barked back at me, but he couldn't get out."

I scowled. "Did you see anybody? Whoever locked him in?"

She shook her head, smearing the tears with the back of her hand. "I didn't see anybody. Will you get him out, Steve?"

"I don't know. If they actually locked the door, I may not be able to. Come on, let's go see."

I stuck the granola bar in my pocket and ate the last of my sandwich on the way over. Sure enough, we could hear Sandy barking before we got there.

I looked in the window. It was fairly dark in there, but I could see Sandy, all right. When we spoke to him, he tried to leap up toward the window, his tail wagging.

"What did he go in there for?" I asked crossly. "Shut up, Sandy, and let me think."

The big doors that opened onto the driveway were locked, sure enough. I went around to the smaller door on the side toward the house. "If this one's locked, too, I don't know anything to do except call the owner and ask him to come over with a key. I doubt if he'll be happy about that. Ah-hah!"

We were in luck. This time. The small door opened when I turned the knob and shoved on it. Sandy came boiling out. He leaped up on me, and when I brought my knee up to fend him off, there were dirty streaks on my jeans again.

I said a few words. More oil. Only this time, I saw by looking past him into the garage, he'd walked through a puddle on the concrete floor inside, so he was really smeared with it.

Now the guy was keeping his leaky car in the garage. It certainly appeared that someone was here regularly. "There's another bag from Rotten Ralphie's. No wonder Sandy comes around." I pulled the door shut, to make sure he didn't get in there again, and said to him, "Come on, bird brain, let's go home."

Once we got there, we cleaned off Sandy's feet before we let him in the house, to make sure he didn't cause any more damage.

The twins came by right after Cindy and Mark and I'd had lunch. Mark wanted to go with us to the movies. Usually when he wanted to go somewhere I said no. He was only ten, and my friends didn't especially appreciate having a little kid along.

The twins said they didn't care, as long as he

kept still, so since Mom was home with Cindy by then, we said Mark could go.

The movie was about some monsters very much like the ones I'd made up. They were dark reddish-purple and had slime dripping off from them, leaving a trail wherever they went. They were extremely well done, we all thought.

"It's a shame they can't have good special effects *and* a plot in the same movie," Ricky said as we walked home. "The story was stupid, but I loved those creatures. Boy, didn't it give you goose bumps along your spine when that thing crawled over Caputo when he was unconscious?"

We stopped at Rotten Ralphie's on the way home for hamburgers. The twins get paid for doing yard work, and I had the paper routes. Mark only gets an allowance, so I paid for his burger. We sat in the park to eat them.

"Boy," Mark said, "Ralphie sure makes good burgers."

We put our sack and the wrappers in a trash barrel. It reminded me of whatever was going on at the old Hanson place, and I told them about it.

"Anybody stupid enough to leave hamburger wrappers lying around," Ray said, "deserves to have his stuff stolen by a dog."

When we passed the house, I looked very carefully. If somebody moved in, I wanted to get there and try to sell them a subscription before anybody else did.

At the corner of Maple and Elm streets there was a condominium going up. There had been a big fight about it, in the city council, because ours was supposed to be a family neighborhood, one family to a house, and this place had eight units. I couldn't help thinking that another eight families all in one building could help me win a big contest. The trick was getting to the tenants first, before Shorty did.

"Looks like it'll be opening soon," Ray observed as we walked past it. "They're finishing up now, aren't they?"

"Yeah. I'm going to talk to Mr. Hubbard and see if he'll give me a list of tenants," I said, having just thought of it. "Maybe I can sign them up before they actually move in." There wasn't time then, though, because I had to deliver the *Herald*.

It hadn't been too bad a day, I thought when I got ready for bed that night. I put in a tape to play while I got tired enough to sleep. Mark was already burrowed under the covers, just a tuft of brown hair sticking out, his back to me. So I didn't think I'd wake him.

If I won that tape-player, I thought, I could

listen to my tapes without worrying about anything because it had an ear plug.

I heard my dad taking a shower. I reached out and pulled the tape out of the player, and then I fell asleep. I woke up sometime later, in pitch blackness, to hear Mark yelling and thumping around before he fell out of bed.

By the time I turned on the light, he was sprawled on the floor, tangled in his blankets, looking dazed and confused.

"Oh, Steve! I'm glad it's you!" he gasped.

"Who did you think it was?" I glanced at the clock; it was a quarter past two.

"I guess I was dreaming. I thought those big slug things were crawling all over me, sucking out my blood—"

He didn't see Dad in the doorway in his pajamas.

"They weren't bloodsuckers, Mark—"

He shuddered. "The ones in my dream were. Boy, it was scary!"

Dad came into the room, frowning. "What's going on? Is Mark having nightmares now, too? Steve, I warned you about scaring the younger kids—"

"Hey! Dad, I didn't do anything to scare him, honest! Mom said to take him along to the movies, and he wanted to go. It's not my fault it was a spooky movie."

"Well, I don't want any more of this. Your mother and I have to get some sleep, understand? Get back in bed, Mark."

I half expected him to add, "And don't have any more nightmares, you hear me?" It wasn't fair to blame me, or maybe not even to blame Mark. How could you help what you dreamed?

After Dad had gone back to bed, I punched my pillow into shape and snarled into the darkness. "See if I take you to any more movies, buddy."

"Aw, come on, Steve!" Mark pleaded. "I can't help it if I have a bad dream."

I knew he was right, but I didn't apologize.

Dad's idea of an ideal Sunday is sitting around eating a lot, watching a ball game on TV, and being waited on. He'll say, "Bring me the paper, will you, Steve?" or to my mom, "Would you make me a sandwich, honey?" or "Cindy, would you get my slippers?"

Everybody but Mom tries to figure out ways to be beyond hearing range. Mark and Cindy went out in the backyard to build Sandy a house—Dad said he tells enough people how to build doghouses so he didn't want to do any himself, and he didn't want a dog in the first place. I figured I'd better find something to do or I'd be the number one servant of the day.

Some of the guys were playing with a Frisbee in the park when I walked over there, and I fooled around with them for an hour or so. I was getting hungry after that, so I thought I'd go home and have something to eat. A Rotten Ralphie's hamburger sounded good, but I decided I really couldn't afford one two days in a row.

That made me think about the leaky car I'd seen at the old Hanson place, so I walked home that way.

To my surprise, there was a dark blue van parked behind the house. And when I bent over to look underneath, sure enough, there was a new puddle of oil.

Just then a guy came out of the garage; he stopped when he saw me. He was about twenty, I guessed, and he was wearing jeans and a white T-shirt. At least, it had been white. There was dirt on the front of it, as if he'd been carrying something dusty.

"You want something?" he asked. He didn't sound friendly. I noticed something interesting, though. He was wearing the watch with the leather strap.

"Uh, no," I said, with the smile I give to potential customers. "I just noticed you've got a bad oil leak."

"So how's that your business?" he snapped.

Wow. So much for being a helpful citizen. "I just thought you might not have noticed. If you don't care, I don't," I said.

Just then another guy came out of the garage. This one was wearing jeans and a dirty T-shirt, too. Instead of being tall and skinny, he was big and fat, and he wore thick horn-rimmed glasses. He didn't look any more friendly than the first guy.

"What's going on?" he wanted to know.

"Some kid. Says we got an oil leak," the skinny one said.

"Yeah? Tell me something I don't know," the fat man said.

They didn't seem like very good prospects, but when you're out to win a contest, it doesn't matter how well you like your patrons. "Are you moving into this house?" I asked. "I deliver papers around here. The morning *Times* and the evening *Herald*. I'd be glad to sign you up for whichever one you prefer."

"We don't read newspapers," the fat one said, and went back into the garage.

I stared after him, then offered a smile to the skinny one, still standing there. "Well, thanks anyway. Tell you what, I could leave you a free paper, let you see what you're missing."

The guy sighed, the way my mom does when she wants to indicate I'm being a pain. "We already told you, we aren't interested."

"You moving in, though?" I asked. "Renting the place?"

"That's not really any of your business, is it?" he asked, and then he went in the garage, too.

Nice neighbors, I thought.

4

I brought up the subject at supper that night. "I guess the old Hanson house isn't haunted, after all," I said. "There's a couple of guys moving into it, is all."

Cindy gave me a panicky look, as if she thought I might mention how Sandy had helped himself to lunch and a watch over there. I knew better than that.

"I tried to sell them a paper, but they said they didn't read newspapers." I reached for another couple of ripe olives. "I don't know if it's worthwhile to leave them a free Sunday paper tomorrow or not. I have one left."

Dad frowned, but for once not at me. "That's

funny. I ran into Harold Hanson at the bowling alley Friday night. I told him you'd mentioned seeing a light or something over there a few days ago. He said there wasn't supposed to be anybody around. He's going to try to sell the place when he gets back from vacation. They're leaving tomorrow, going to Bermuda for a month. I asked him why he didn't have Cliff handle it, if he was staying home."

"Who's Cliff?" Mark asked.

"Cliff's his son. Works for Harold at the body shop, I think. Harold just made a snorting noise. I asked if he was going to fix the place up first, paint it and so on, and he said no. He was going to list it as is. Funny he didn't say anything about renting it. I mean, it doesn't make sense to rent it if you're going to try to sell it in a month."

It *was* odd that those two guys were moving into a house that was going to be sold in a matter of weeks. Come to think of it, they hadn't actually said they were renting it, though. The skinny one had said it was none of my business.

It's sort of funny, how when somebody tells you something is none of your business, it makes you more curious than you were before. At least that was how it worked with me.

Maybe I had a funny look on my face, because

Dad gave *me* one of his looks. "Don't work it up into anything, all right, Steve?"

"Huh? What do you—"

"What I mean is, don't make a big deal out of nothing just to sound interesting, all right? I know you like to get the little kids stirred up, but let's have no more of this monsters in the closet stuff, including no ghosts in haunted houses. OK? The next kid that has a nightmare in this family," he grinned so we'd know he was making one of his heavy jokes, "loses out on dessert for a week. Even if we're having chocolate cake."

"Hey!" Mark cried. "That's not fair, Dad! Mom, he can't really take our dessert because of a nightmare, can he?"

She gave Dad one of those looks that means he's as bad as the kids, and put a slice of cake in front of Mark. "All right, the whole bunch of you, forget it. Eat."

Still I couldn't help thinking about those guys at the Hanson house, even if nobody would let me talk about them.

I left a copy of the *Times* on the porch, with a slip of paper held on by the rubber band. I wrote a note on the paper:

"This is a courtesy copy for your enjoyment. If

you'd like to subscribe, call me at 847-3224. Your *Times* carrier, Steve Quentin."

I didn't really think they'd take a subscription, but it would give me an excuse to go back there. There was something fishy about those two guys and their leaking car.

Monday was a bad day. I had delivered all the papers except the one to the Sarellas, which I never liked doing because they had this big Doberman named Hercules. He never bothered me as long as I threw the paper from outside the gate, but if I didn't manage to get it onto the porch, he'd tear it to shreds on the lawn. Mr. Sarella always deducted the price of any paper that had been torn from my bill, which wasn't exactly fair. They wouldn't let me enter the yard, because they couldn't take a chance on Hercules getting out, and it was a long throw.

That morning Hercules surprised me, bounding out of the shrubbery just as I was about to throw. He startled me enough so the throw was bad, and the paper landed on the sidewalk in front of the steps.

I looked at it and pictured the confetti it would be when Mr. Sarella came out to get his paper half an hour from now. The words I thought were not nice words. Hercules twisted in midair and headed for the newspaper.

"No, Hercules!" I yelled. "Drop it! Drop it! Bad dog!"

He knew the words "bad dog." He stood over the paper as if guarding it, looking at me uncertainly.

It didn't take long to figure out I was part of a stalemate. The minute I turned my back, that darned dog was going to have a ball with that paper.

I yelled again, hoping maybe one of the Sarellas would hear me and come out. Nothing happened.

I could either let Hercules have it, or go in and take it away from him.

I'd never tried to rescue a misthrown paper from him before. Although Hercules barked and jumped up at the fence, he'd never acted as if he meant to bite me. He *knew* me.

I put the stand down on my bike and moved toward the gate. The idea was to make him think I had a right to walk in there and pick up the paper. I opened the gate and was inside, with it latched behind me, before Hercules decided I wasn't behaving according to the rules.

I walked straight at him, saying, "Sit, boy. Sit,

39

Hercules," the way I'd heard Mr. Sarella doing.

He sat all right. He waited until I got within a foot of him and then he growled.

A full grown Doberman, growling, is enough to make anybody reconsider their plans. I stopped, feeling a knot form in the pit of my stomach. "Good boy," I said.

From the look in his yellowish eyes, I didn't think he believed what I'd just said.

I started, very slowly, to bend over and reach for the paper. He growled again.

"Oh, come on, now," I said, trying to sound authoritative. "I have to get home and have breakfast and go to school, so don't hold me up, OK?"

I decided it might be safer to move the paper away from him with my foot, than to get my face down there by his. I stuck out a foot and put it on the end of the newspaper. So far so good. Hercules was just watching me.

"Lie down," I said. "Down, boy."

Ever so slowly, Hercules lowered his rump to the sidewalk, then followed with his front quarters, but the paper was still between his front paws.

"Stay," I told him. I eased my foot back, bringing the paper with it. He looked at it as if this might be some sort of game, and in a minute it would be his turn to retrieve it.

I said, "Stay, Hercules," again, and picked up the paper.

I had drawn back to throw, when I saw that he wasn't going to stay. Just as I let go, he leaped.

I can throw a paper pretty much where I want it, except when a Doberman has hold of my pant leg. He wasn't hurting me, at least not so far, but I heard his teeth go through my jeans. It threw me off, so the paper went wild.

There was the sound of breaking glass, and Hercules tried to shake my pant leg as if it were a big rat he'd captured. He still wasn't biting, though he wasn't letting me go, either. I was glad when Mr. Sarella appeared in the front doorway in his bathrobe and demanded to know what was going on.

I would have thought it was obvious. His dog was trying to kill me. Luckily, he yelled at Hercules, who finally let go. I looked down and saw big teeth marks in my pants.

It wasn't a window that had broken, but the globe over the porch light. I wondered if he'd expect me to pay for it, and decided that if he did, I'd give him the bill for a new pair of jeans.

"What happened?" Mr. Sarella asked. He shook his head when I explained. "After this, don't come in the yard. You're lucky he didn't hurt you. He bit the gas man last week."

41

He didn't say anything about paying for the light globe, so I didn't say anything about my pants. I got out the gate while he held Hercules, and went on home, feeling lucky to have escaped with my life.

I was telling Mark about it when Dad came down. He said, "For pete's sake, Steve, do you have to try to scare somebody to death every time you open your mouth?"

It sort of spoiled my pancakes, which I'd been looking forward to. I didn't think it was fair that I couldn't even talk about something that really happened.

The day went downhill from there. When I got to school, I discovered I'd left my English composition at home, and Mrs. Field acted as if she didn't believe I'd actually done it. We had a surprise quiz in Current Events, and since I'd been too busy delivering papers to read any of them, I missed six questions. I passed, but I didn't get what you'd call a good grade.

At lunch they had creamed codfish and peas on toast. I took one bite and put down my fork. I ate the carrot sticks and the milk and apple crisp, and I was still hungry.

We played soccer during P.E. and I wasn't lucky there, either. Somehow or other, I managed to get knocked down just when Ricky was kicking the ball, and he got me in the face. I had a bloody nose and the coach insisted I go see the school nurse, though I told him it would stop before I got to her office.

It did, but I still had to sit there and listen to her explain to some dopey kid that she couldn't go home just because she was tired and she had a hangnail, or something.

I was glad when the day was over.

Ricky and Ray were waiting for me when I came out the front door at three-thirty. "Hey, we have to go get haircuts. Why don't you walk down to the barber shop with us?" Ray said.

After I left them off, I headed toward home, and because I took a short cut I saw this shop I'd never noticed before.

It was on a side street, and it said Henry's Electronics, Video and Stereo. There was a big home-made sign—Mark could have done better lettering—in the front window, that said SALE! CASSETTE TAPES, HALF PRICE.

I was always looking for bargains, so I went in to look around. It wasn't as nice a place as Smitty's, but there was a bin with tapes in it. I started looking through them.

Wow, I thought. There was an album by the

Montana Magnets that I'd been looking for, and one by Jimmy Joe and the Jubees I'd had once and somebody swiped it. I'd always wanted a replacement.

"Help you, kid?"

The man who ran the place was watching me. He was going bald, and he wore glasses he had to squint through to see me.

"You got some good tapes," I said. "I'll be back after I collect for my papers this month. I don't suppose you could save any of them for me?"

"No need. There'll be plenty. I sell cheaper than anybody else in town."

I nodded. "I can see that. It's a good price."

"You bet." He grinned. "Tell your friends, kid."

"OK, I will."

I picked up my papers and made my rounds, glad the Sarellas didn't take the *Herald*. All I needed to make the day complete was another encounter with Hercules.

5

There was a rolled-up sleeping bag by our front door, an overnight bag standing next to it, and a Tupperware container that looked as if it were full of cookies on top of the bag.

"What's going on?" I wanted to know.

Dad was reading the paper. And Mark was painting a sign to go over the door of Sandy's doghouse. I was surprised nobody'd made him do it in the garage, even if he did have newspapers all over the floor to protect the carpet.

I took the top off the Tupperware container and helped myself to a couple of chocolate chip cookies.

"You better leave those alone," Mark warned.

"Cindy's taking them to a slumber party at Betsy's."

I bit off half of one. "They wouldn't want me to put these back, not with my germs on them. What're we having for supper?"

"Roast beef," Mark said. I knew he'd have checked out the menu as soon as Mom started cooking. "Braised potatoes, salad, and brussel sprouts. Jell-O for dessert. Red, with bananas in it."

I debated whether I could get away with taking a third cookie and decided not. Cindy was coming down the stairs.

She was staggering under the weight of another handbag and clutching a pillow in the other hand.

"I thought this was a slumber party, for one night. You look as if you're going for a week," I told her.

"I'm taking my records," Cindy said, putting the second bag down with a sigh of relief. "Everybody's taking something to eat, and their records."

"You ought to have tapes," I advised. "They're easier to carry. Is somebody giving you a ride, I hope?"

"Nancy's mother is going to pick me up at six-thirty. Mark, you won't forget to feed Sandy, will you?"

"Nope," Mark agreed, putting the final touches

to the board with the dog's name on it. For a kid who's such a slob in so many ways, he did a neat job of lettering, freehand.

"You better feed him," I offered. "Otherwise, he'll eat whatever comes along. The mailman, the dog from across the street, somebody's garbage."

"He'd better learn to stay away from garbage," Dad said from behind the newspaper, "ours, or anybody else's, if he wants to continue to live at our house."

Cindy gave me a reproachful glance for bringing up the subject. I tried to make it up to her. "I'll carry all this stuff out to the car when Nancy's mother gets here. How come you're having a slumber party on a school night, anyway?"

"It's Betsy's birthday. We've promised to go to sleep at nine o'clock," Cindy explained.

Mark and I looked at each other. Since when would a bunch of little girls stop giggling and go to sleep as soon as Betsy's mother turned off the lights.

"Be thankful," Mark said, "that it's not at *our* house."

I had to go out and see the doghouse before supper. It wasn't bad, considering. The only trouble was that Sandy didn't want to go in it, even though Cindy had put dog biscuits in there.

47

"He stuck his head in and got the biscuits, but we couldn't push him inside," Mark said. "Dad says if he gets cold enough, or wet enough, he'll go in."

Nancy's mother came just as we were finishing our dessert. I carried the stuff out to the station wagon and piled Cindy's sleeping bag and suitcase in with the other ones already there. I heard the little girls whispering and giggling, and, like Mark, I was glad they weren't having the slumber party at our house.

That didn't mean I had a nice quiet evening, though. At least not for the whole evening. I did my homework and read and listened to some music until about eight o'clock; by that time I was hungry, so I went downstairs and made myself a sandwich of the leftover roast with mustard and lettuce and onions.

I was at the foot of the stairs when the phone rang.

Dad was reading a western and Mom was reading a mystery. They both looked at me and said, "Get that, will you, Steve?"

The phone was on a stand at the bottom of the stairs. I put down my tray and said, "Hello? Quentin residence."

"Steve? This is Betsy Thole's father," said a deep

voice.

"Yes, sir," I said. Instinctively, I turned my back to my folks. "This is Steve." When I said that, my parents went back to their reading. They were used to me getting phone calls in the evening, because of the paper routes.

"We have a problem here," Mr. Thole said. "It's about that dog."

I lowered my voice. "Sandy?"

"I guess that's what she called him, yes. Overgrown Great Dane pup, by the look of him. The girls have found him to be very entertaining, but we want them to calm down and go to sleep." He sounded about the way I'd expect Dad to sound under those circumstances. Unhappy. "The thing is, they aren't going to sleep with that dog here. I wonder if you'd mind taking him home."

"Yes, sir, of course. I'll be right over," I agreed. I looked regretfully at my sandwich.

"Forget someone?" Mom asked.

"Not exactly," I said. "I have to go out, though. It's over on Cedar Street. I'll only be gone a few minutes."

"Take a flashlight," Mom said.

Mark was fixing his own bedtime snack when I went back to the kitchen for the flashlight. He had a sandwich that nobody's mouth could ever get around—to my basic ingredients he'd added cheese and tomatoes and a couple of slices of left-over bacon—and he wanted to know where I was going.

"Over to Tholes' to bring back Sandy. What I want to know is how he got over there. If you left the gate unlatched again, I may brain you."

"I didn't!" Mark protested. He added a couple of pickle slices to his sandwich and put the top slice of bread on it. "Go look, if you don't believe me."

"Let's both look," I suggested, so he left his sandwich, too, and we went outside.

The gate to the alley was latched, as it was supposed to be, and so was the one that led to the walk around the side of the house. The answer was there though. Right beside the gate was a mound of fresh dirt where Sandy had dug under the fence.

Mark looked at the hole. "He heard Cindy leaving, and he tunneled out and followed the car. The way Nancy's mother drives, anybody could follow her. She never gets over fifteen miles an hour."

He decided he wanted to come with me, so we both put our sandwiches on hold and took off.

We could hear the laughter when we went up the steps to the Tholes' front door. Cindy brought the dog out to us. "I'm sorry, Steve. I didn't know he was behind us until we got here, and then Betsy said let him in to play with. Everything was OK until Mr. Thole heard him barking."

Dad had brought home a leash for him, along with a collar, so I clipped on the chain and we started for home.

It was a nice night. Sandy ambled along, pausing from time to time to smell something interesting, like a tree or a fire hydrant or nothing in particular.

"You know what? There was a van at the Hanson house today," Mark said. "I saw it on my way home from school."

"That right? Was it leaking oil?"

"I didn't get close enough to see. It was behind the house. It was old, though, dark blue. There were three guys standing around it."

"Three, huh? I only saw two." I described them. "What did the third one look like?"

Mark shrugged. "Just a guy. He was wearing a plaid cap, and he wasn't either skinny or fat, just medium. I couldn't tell what they were doing."

"Probably bank robbers or something," I said. "Using the place for a hideout. Who else would move in when it's going to be put up for sale in a month?"

"Bank robbers. Yeah," Mark agreed. "That's probably it. Have there been any bank robberies lately?"

"I don't know. I haven't had time to read anything but the front pages and the funnies lately. But there's always bank robberies. That place would be a good hideout. Nobody can see into the yard through all that thick hedge, and the house is far back from the street. They could be doing anything, and nobody would see it."

"Yeah," Mark agreed, with rising enthusiasm. "What do you think they're doing, Steve?"

"Maybe they're counterfeiters," I said. "Maybe that's why they put cardboard over the basement windows, because they've put their operation down there and don't want anybody to see in."

"You mean making money? What's it take to counterfeit money? A printing press?"

"A printing press, and maybe a table where they draw out the bills. They have to make up plates, before they can print. Whatever it is they're doing in there, I'll bet it's illegal."

"You think Mr. Harold Hanson knows what's going on there?"

"No. He's what Dad calls a solid citizen."

Sandy jerked sideways on the leash, and I nearly tripped over my own feet trying to keep up with him. "Come on, Sandy! Cut it out," I said crossly, pulling him back.

"Listen, Steve, let's go past the Hanson house and see if anything's going on there, OK?"

I thought about my snack waiting for me, but what the heck? It would only take a couple of extra minutes to go that way. I cut across the street, Mark running to keep up.

"If Mr. Hanson doesn't know what's going on, how do you suppose they got in? They have keys, don't they?"

"I guess so. It didn't look as if the doors had been kicked in. Hey, there're lights in the Evergreen Arms." That was the condominium. "Let's stop and see if it's Mr. Hubbard. Maybe they're getting ready to let people move in."

Mr. Hubbard was the contractor who had built the place. I knew him because he was one of my customers. He came over and opened the glass door when I knocked on it.

"Hi, kids. What's that you've got, a pony?"

"No, he's a dog," Mark said. "A Great Dane."

"You could have fooled me. What can I do for you?"

"I wondered if you'd give me a list of tenants—

you know, the people who are going to move in pretty soon? I want to sell them some newspapers. I need new customers for the current contest."

"Oh. Well." He scratched his nearly bald head. "I don't have a list, but my wife does. Tell you what, I'll mention it to her, and you can stop when you deliver tomorrow's paper. How'll that be?"

"Thanks, Mr. Hubbard," I told him.

He laughed. "I'll expect not to find my paper in the rhododendron bushes anymore, all right?"

"It's a promise," I told him, and figured it would be worth the little extra effort, if I signed up all eight tenants.

I don't know if Mark expected to see anything while we were going past the Hanson house. I know I didn't.

But there it was again. A light at the rear of the house.

Mark let out a long breath. "Hey! They're doing *something*, Steve. Let's sneak around and see if we can tell what it is!"

We moved silently along the sidewalk. And when we rounded the corner of the house, there was a flashlight.

I heard the voice of the fat man.

"Come on, get the door open, will you? And stop waving that light around. Somebody'll see it."

The guy with the watch was standing just a few yards away with his back to us, holding a paper bag. "Hurry up, Eddie, let's get unloaded and eat. I'm starved."

The light didn't touch the bag enough so I could be sure what it was, but almost at once I smelled it—hamburgers with onions. And so did Sandy.

He whined and strained against the leash.

I knew then how stupid I'd been, to head right up close to them with that darned dog.

6

Sandy lunged forward, straight at that familiar paper bag that was giving off a mouth-watering aroma. I wasn't expecting him to pull that way, and he jerked the leash right out of my hand.

I heard the skinny guy yell and saw him throw up the arm holding the sack. He wasn't fast enough: Sandy tore the bottom out of it, spilling hamburgers and french fries onto the ground.

The fat guy yelled, too, and dropped the carton he was carrying. Sandy grabbed one foil-wrapped hamburger and ran right between the legs of the guy who still held the top of the empty bag, sending the man sprawling backward.

The light bobbed around, trying to follow Sandy.

I caught a glimpse of the fat man, and of a dark blue van, and then the flashlight beam swept back to silhouette Mark.

"Run!" I hissed.

I bolted toward the street; it was a few seconds before I realized the only sound I heard—except for my heart pounding—was my own feet thudding on the grass. Not Mark's.

I spun around. One of the men started to swear. There was no sign of Sandy. He'd gotten away, but the three men were converging on Mark.

He stood there as if he'd grown roots. They had the flashlight shining right in his face.

"What are you doing here?" the fat man demanded. He was the one called Eddie, I thought. "How come you're snooping around?"

"I—I—I—" Mark stammered. "I was chasing my dog. He got away from me. I—I—I— guess he smelled your hamburgers."

Skinny-with-the-watch crumpled up what was left of the paper bag and threw it on the ground. "He got away with one of 'em, and the french fries are all spilled out. It's the same dog that got our lunch before! Listen, kid." He reached out and grabbed Mark by the front of his shirt. I started toward them, though I didn't know what I was going to do, not against three men.

The guy was shaking Mark so that his head wobbled. "You keep that dog away from here, you understand? I'm not losing any more food to that dog!"

He gave Mark a final shake and pushed him backward; Mark sprawled on his back, and I stopped where I was, beyond the range of the flashlight. It didn't look as if they intended to do any more than frighten Mark. I'd have to jump into the middle of it if they touched him again, but I didn't like the idea of being beaten up by three men. I hoped he'd get up.

They gathered up the remaining hamburgers— still wrapped —and the light swung back around to where the fat man was picking up the carton · he'd dropped. I couldn't see the fellow holding the flashlight, but he seemed more interested in rescuing what he could of the food than in chasing anybody.

Mark scrambled around and got to his feet; he ran right into me in the dark. "It's OK, they're not coming after us. Come on, let's get out of here."

"I thought they were going to kill me," he gasped. We trotted toward the street, not feeling safe until we were under the streetlights and beyond the hedge.

"I thought you'd run away and left me, Steve."

"No, I wouldn't do that," I assured him. I was beginning to feel I hadn't been very brave, though I didn't really see what else I could have done. "I'd have started yelling if they'd touched you again. Maybe Mrs. Constantine next door would have heard me and called the police, the way she always does when the kids play noisy games on the other side of her house."

Mark was getting his breath back. "What happened to Sandy?"

"He got one of the hamburgers and ran for the alley. He probably ate it, foil and all."

"I suppose we ought to go down the alley and see if we can find him, then."

"I guess so," I agreed. "Then when we get home we'll have to fill in the hole under the fence. I don't know how we're going to keep him from digging out again, though. Maybe we'll have to keep him tied up."

"Do you think Dad will let us keep him," Mark asked, "if he has to be tied? He thinks you shouldn't have dogs unless they can run and exercise."

"This one's getting plenty of exercise," I said grimly. "And so am I. Let's cut through behind Lindquist's place; they're both deaf, so *they* shouldn't hear us and call the cops."

We didn't find Sandy in the alley. He was in his

new doghouse, a few tattered bits of lettuce and foil between his front paws.

He wagged his tail as if he were happy to see us, which is more than I could say for seeing him. We went inside, got our snacks, and heard Mom call, "Time to head for the showers, boys," as we started up the stairs.

I was sure curious about those three guys at the Hanson house. Whatever they were up to, it was something shady, I knew it was. And I intended to find out what.

I thought Mark was never going to calm down and go to sleep. I was listening to Rudy Plum and the Pits, turned down low so Mom wouldn't hear it, and trying to get another chapter or two read on my mystery. Just about the time I'd pick up the thread of the story, Mark would flop over and say something.

"Steve? What do you think those guys are doing over there?"

"I already told you. I think they're crooks of some kind," I said, still trying to read.

"You think they're dangerous?"

"Well, I wouldn't take any chances with them. They might be."

"I mean, if they robbed a bank or were counterfeiting, you think they might be killers, too?"

"Who knows? Don't go around there, Mark. Stay away from them. Dad would be mad if he knew, even about tonight."

"How are we going to find out what they're doing if we don't go around there?"

"I didn't say *I* wasn't going to keep on investigating. I told *you* to stay away from there."

Mark lay back on the pillow with his hands behind his head. "If they're bank robbers, and you find out where they stashed the money, you think they'll have a reward?"

I grinned. "They might."

"How much? How much you think they'd give us, if we got their money back for them?"

"We? You're not going with me, if I go investigating."

Mark thought that over. "I think you're making a mistake."

I reached for the light. "Go to sleep, Mark."

In the dark I heard him breathing. "Steve? If they got back, say, fifty thousand dollars, would they give you one thousand dollars reward?"

"Oh, at least. Be nice, having a thousand dollars, wouldn't it?"

"Boy, yeah. You think we could get one of those electronic games? Intellivision, or Atari?"

"What good would it do us? You have to play it on a TV. You think Dad's going to give up watching ball games so we can play Pac Man or Space Invaders?"

He sighed. "No, I guess not." Then he brightened. "Maybe we could get our own TV. Keep it up here."

"Sure, why not? Goodnight, Mark."

He finally did shut up, then. I lay there in the darkness, thinking about it. It wouldn't be bad at all, getting the evidence on a bunch of crooks. The police would arrest them, and the bank would give us a reward, and probably the *Times* and the *Herald* would both do stories on it. Front page, maybe. With my picture. Mark's, too, of course, if he was in on it.

The problem was how to get the evidence without getting hurt myself. I didn't want to be a hero so bad that I was willing to risk getting hurt.

I hadn't thought of any answer to that before I fell asleep.

I guess I dreamed about having a fight with the big fat one, Eddie. I thought he was sitting on me, pounding me with a pillow that didn't actually hurt but was scaring me half to death.

I woke up sort of gasping for breath, the way you do when you come out of a bad dream, then it seemed like a bad dream, being awake. Had I cried out? Had Dad heard? I lay stiff and listening, waiting for Dad to come. But he didn't. I finally let out my breath.

It took me a while to fall asleep again. I kept wondering how dangerous those guys were, and if I'd be risking more than nightmares if I went back to the Hanson house.

7

I told the Swan twins about it the next day. We walked downtown together after school. They had some birthday money they wanted to spend, and I told them about the shop where I'd seen the sale on tapes.

"Gee," Ray said when I'd related the whole tale, "you think they're really dangerous, Steve?"

"I don't know. But I sure want to find out what they're up to."

"Listen," Ricky said, "there was no sign of breaking in, so they must have keys, right? Where did they get the keys if they didn't rent the place?"

"I don't know. Maybe they stole them."

"You said Sandy kept going for their lunch bags," Ray mused. "Why don't you ask Ralphie if he knows who they are? I mean, if they keep buying hamburgers from him, maybe he knows them."

I hit my forehead with my fist. "Why didn't I think of that? I'll ask him next time I get over there. Today, though, I've got to make collections, and see Mrs. Hubbard for a list of the people moving into that condo."

"You say there are three of those guys," Ricky said, "and there are three of us. Maybe we could all investigate."

"I'm not going to help tackle three men," Ray objected. "I'm not crazy, even if you two are."

"I don't mean get into an open confrontation with them," Ricky said. "I meant, we could help Steve find out. For instance, are they really living there? Or just doing something there at night?"

I shrugged. "Who knows? What're we going to do, have a stakeout, like the cops?"

Ricky was getting more enthusiastic. "Sure, why not? We could find out if they're there all the time or only in the evening. And then when they're gone, we could try to get in and see what they're doing there!"

"That's breaking and entering," Ray pointed out. "It's a felony."

"Well, what if what *they're* doing is a felony, too? We wouldn't have to break in, maybe we could learn something without going that far. Anyway, what do you think? It wouldn't hurt to observe for a night, would it? Maybe we could find out what's going on just by watching from outside." He thought about it. "You could hide an army under that hedge, once it's dark, and nobody'd see it. So we could sneak in after dark—we'd have to wait until kind of late, so our folks would think we'd all gone to sleep—and see what happens."

We talked about it some more, and it sounded like a good idea. "Only we'd better wait until Friday," Ray said, "so if we're up all night we can sleep in on Saturday morning."

We agreed to that, and by then we'd reached the little electronic shop. They bought six tapes apiece—at half-price, they could afford to—and I broke down and bought one. "I'll be back after I make my collections this month and get some more money," I told the proprietor.

He grinned. "Tell all your friends—cheapest tapes in town."

As we headed for the front door, somebody came in from the back. I took one look and hurried after the twins. "Did you see who just came in?"

"No, who?"

"Some fat guy," Ricky observed, looking back over his shoulder.

"Yeah. The fat guy that's fooling around the Hanson place. One of the other guys called him Eddie."

Ricky stopped, looking back through the window, until Ray pulled on his arm.

"Come on. Don't call attention to us, you dope."

"Wonder what he's doing here?"

"Buying some cheap tapes, maybe. These really are a bargain, Steve. Thanks for telling us about them."

They took their tapes home to play them. Mine had to wait. I picked up my papers early, as I usually did when I had collections to make, and went home long enough to get something to eat. I always had to fortify myself for the ordeal.

It wasn't only that it always took me so long I was late for supper. The worst of it was the frustration of not getting paid the first time I called.

That day was no worse than usual. Mrs. Gardner said she hadn't had a chance to cash her pension check yet, and Mr. Floramunda said he'd spent everything at the emergency room and couldn't pay me until he got paid next week. He was wearing a cast on his left arm, so I guessed that excuse was genuine. Everybody else paid me.

Mrs. Hubbard, the contractor's wife, had written out a list of the new tenants for the condo. "They're mostly elderly people," she said. "I should think they'd all want newspapers. I put down the current telephone numbers for the ones that live on the other side of town now. I thought maybe you'd want to contact them that way instead of riding your bike so far."

I thanked her and headed on home. There I decided to call a couple of them and see how I made out. The first three I called subscribed to the *Times,* the next one took both papers. "Got nothing to do but read papers and watch TV," he said.

The rest of them were in my own neighborhood already. I'd see them in person when I was delivering close to them. I hoped Shorty Bergen didn't have a condo going up in his territory.

It was Thursday before I managed to get over to Rotten Ralphie's after school. I slid onto a stool at the counter, figuring I'd better buy something, just to put him in a cooperative mood. Not that he wasn't, usually.

He rested big freckled arms on the counter and looked at me. "Hi, Steve. What'll you have?"

"A Jumbo, I guess. With an orange soda." I

waited until he was cooking it before I put the crucial question. "Ralphie, I'm trying to identify somebody. Maybe you could help me."

He looked around from the grill and grinned. "You playing detective?"

"Sort of." My dad never came in here, so I figured it was safe to tell Ralphie the story of our dog swiping the hamburgers. I embellished it a little, made it sound funnier than it really was. I left out everything about the peculiar activities at the Hanson house, and didn't mention it by name.

He laughed. "Your dog has good taste. So do your mysterious friends. Tell me what they look like."

I described the two I'd seen clearly, adding that the third was just a young fellow, neither fat nor thin.

Ralphie scratched his chin. "Don't sound familiar. Let me ask the girls."

There were about half a dozen high school girls working for him at any given time. Several of the girls were waiting on other customers. Three came over to hear me repeat my descriptions.

One of them shook her head. The other two exchanged glances.

"Sound like those guys who were in here the

other night with Cliff Hanson. Remember? Cliff called one *Eddie*. The fat one. Who was the third one?"

I practically froze on the stool. "Cliff Hanson?" I hadn't expected that. Did that mean they had a right to be there, after all? It didn't prove that what the men were doing was legitimate, though, I thought.

"I'm pretty sure it was him," the girl said. "They've been coming in regularly for more than a week. Always have the same order. Six hamburgers with everything, three large fries."

"The other guy is new in town, I think," the second girl said. "They called him Harry."

Ralphie stood poised with my hamburger balanced in one hand on a piece of waxed paper, a spatula in the other. "You want this to go, Steve?"

"Yeah, I guess so." I needed to think. "Thanks," I said.

I was thinking so hard I forgot to enjoy the burger as I walked home. It had been worth the price, though. I'd learned something valuable.

I stopped by the Swan house and found the twins doing homework. I knew that meant Mrs. Swan was home, so I kept my voice down. "I found out who the guys are," I said.

When I'd explained it, they both looked at me. "Cliff Hanson. No wonder they have keys."

"I'll bet his folks don't know it," Ray said. "Seems to me Mr. Hanson would have said something to Steve's dad, when Mr. Quentin asked about the place, if he'd known his son was using it. And Cliff lives at home, doesn't he? So he wouldn't need to rent a place, unless he was doing something he didn't want his father to know about."

Before I left, we agreed to meet on the corner by the Hanson house at ten-thirty the following night, to begin our surveillance.

I could hardly wait.

8

All the time I was delivering papers on Friday morning, I kept thinking about staking out the Hanson house that night.

It was raining and I worried about that. I didn't especially look forward to lying under the hedge in the rain for hours. I suspected the twins wouldn't like it any better than I did.

By the time I got to school, though, it had cleared off and the sun was shining.

I got an A in my English test, and a B+ on my math quiz, and we had pizza for lunch. Ricky brought his tray over to my table and unloaded it, with Ray right behind him.

"You all ready for tonight?" I asked, lowering

my voice so the kids at the other end of the table wouldn't hear.

"We're ready," Ray said. "Ten-thirty, right?"

"Right," Ricky and I said together.

Ricky sat down across from me and took a bite of pizza. "Did you find out anything more about Cliff Hanson?"

"No. What's there to find out?"

"We brought up the subject at home. Dad knows *his* dad, and we asked if Cliff still worked at Hanson's Body Shop. He doesn't."

"So?" I tried the pizza. It was better than usual, lots of mushrooms and sausage and cheese. "What's that got to do with anything?"

"Well," Ricky said, "doesn't it seem funny that his own dad would fire him? If I was working for my dad, I don't know what it would take to make him *fire* me."

"Yeah," Ray agreed. "I mean, Dad would *yell* at us a lot, but he wouldn't *fire* us."

"Unless we did something terrible," Ricky said.

"Like steal," Ray added.

I stared at them. "You mean he stole something, from his own father?"

"Well," Ricky conceded, "we don't know for sure, so maybe we shouldn't say it, but he did *something* that cost him his job."

I thought about my dad and his "joke" about nightmares and dessert. He'd fired regular employees for stealing a couple of times. I supposed he'd fire Mark or me, too, if we were working for him and he found out we were thieves. "I don't know Mr. Hanson very well. I don't know what he'd do."

"Well, we found out Cliff Hanson got a job at a gas station, and he only lasted two weeks there. He got fired twice in about a month, once by his own father. So maybe he's the kind of guy who'd get mixed up in something shady."

"It doesn't prove anything," I said.

"No, but it's evidence, isn't it? Circumstantial evidence, that's what they call it. Now we need to get some real evidence, the kind we can take to the police," Ricky said.

"Something's just occurred to me." Ray poked a fork into his salad. "His father may not be very happy with us if we prove his son is mixed up in something crooked. We may get in trouble ourselves."

"The way I look at it," I told them, "is that if something illegal is going on, it's a good citizen's duty to report it. I doubt if his folks would want him to get away with doing something illegal."

"Some parents cover up for their kids," Ray said.

"They'd rather the kid got away with something than to make a scandal and have everybody in town know about it."

"If Cliff is doing something that's harmful to other people," Ricky decided, "he deserves to be caught, whether his father wants a scandal or not. You think maybe they're into drugs or something like that, Steve?"

I thought about it. "I don't know. I doubt it. That fat Eddie was carrying cartons into the house. I never heard of anybody handling drugs that way, in medium sized boxes."

We talked about what it could be that Cliff and Eddie and the guy called Harry were dealing in. There was no way of telling until we got a look inside the old house, we decided.

I met Shorty Bergen in the hallway between P.E. and study hall. He stopped, so I did, too.

"How many customers you got now?" he wanted to know.

"I'm still working on it," I said. I wasn't going to tell him. If I had him beat by one, he'd subscribe to it himself to win the prize.

"You have to turn them in by Monday, you know."

"Sure, I read the rules," I said.

"Well, you can read my name in the paper on

Wednesday, when it says I won the tape-player," he said, sort of cocky.

It wasn't going to be his name at the top of the winners' list if I could help it, I thought. I went into the counselor's office and asked Mr. Biteman if he'd like to subscribe to the *Times*.

"I already take the *Herald*," he said. "Shorty Bergen delivers it every evening."

"You're missing a lot, not getting the *Times*, too," I told him. Dad would have said it wasn't ethical to try to talk him into changing from Shorty's route to mine, and besides, Mr. Biteman's house wasn't in my territory. School wasn't Shorty's territory, though. "I could bring it to you when I come to school," I suggested. "The *Times* really has better coverage of current events. It has about twenty more pages, and part of those are filled with syndicated columnists."

"Is that right," Mr. Biteman said.

"Tell you what. I'll leave you a free copy on Monday and you can compare them. See if you don't think there's a lot you're missing by not getting the *Times*."

He grinned a little. "OK. Leave me a free copy."

I tried the same tactic on the principal, Mrs. Peters, and the vice-principal, Mr. Jacobsmeyer. I didn't make an outright sale, but they both agreed to read the free copy, so I stopped at the nurse's office, too. I knew that sometimes she had a lot of illnesses and accidents to deal with, and sometimes all she had to do was sit and read if her paperwork was caught up.

She considered the matter. "Well, why not? That would mean there'd be something to read even if I forgot to bring a book from home," she said. I signed her up on the spot.

By that time I'd missed half an hour of study hall, so rather than go in late and have to explain where I'd been, I went into the library and did my homework. After school I contacted the rest of the people on the condo list; I wound up with subscriptions from all of the prospective tenants, though two of them wanted the *Herald* instead of the *Times*. That only gave me six more customers, and I was afraid it wasn't going to be enough.

We had barbecued spare ribs for supper, my favorite. I smelled them when I walked in. Cindy met me, beaming. "I made the dessert," she announced.

Mark looked up from a page of long division he was struggling with. "Yuck!" he said.

"If you don't like it, you don't have to eat it," Cindy told him crossly. "Steve can have your share."

"What is it?"

"You wouldn't be interested," she told him, and then, to me, "It's a carrot cake, Steve. With cream cheese frosting."

"Sounds great," I told her. "How's Sandy? Did he stay in the yard today?"

"Oh, yes. Mark and I got some boards to put across the bottom of the fence in the place where he dug out. We don't think he can get out again."

"Come on," said Mark, "let's go eat. I hear Mom opening the oven."

I didn't know how he could hear something that didn't make any more noise than opening the oven, but he was right. She was putting the food on the table. I poured the milk, and Mark filled the bread basket. Dad showed up as we were about to sit down.

Cindy's cake looked sort of lopsided; they'd had to hold it together with toothpicks to keep the top layer from sliding off. She was smiling with pride, though, when she cut it, and Mark was stupid enough to make a remark about how it looked.

"You mean that's a cake? It looks like an accident."

She cut him a slice, and then one for me. Mine was twice as big. It was delicious. I grinned at Mark when he took his first bite.

He eyed the slice on my plate, what was left of it. "How come Steve gets a bigger piece?"

Cindy looked him in the eye. "No seconds on dessert, right, Mom?"

"That's right," Mom agreed. "And next time maybe your brother will use better judgment with his remarks."

It was my turn to clear the table and load the dishwasher. After that I went upstairs to read for a while, if I could, before it was time to pretend to go to bed.

I wasn't exactly nervous, only a little wound up. I put on the new tape I'd bought that week, thinking maybe the music would be soothing.

It didn't seem to soothe Mom. She came to the doorway, all dressed up, and looked at the label on the tape. "Johnny Thunder and the Lightning Bolts? That's the name of a musical group?"

"Good music, huh?" I asked. Then, because I could tell by her face she didn't like the music any better than the name, I changed the subject. "You going somewhere?"

"Does anybody ever listen to me? I mentioned it at suppertime. I'm going to a shower for Laurie, at Aunt Lucille's."

"Oh, yeah. I forgot. Well, have a good time."

"See that Cindy goes to bed at eight, and Mark at nine, all right? Your dad's watching a ball game; unless he runs out of food he won't be paying any attention to you kids."

I sincerely hoped he wouldn't be. "Sure, Mom. I'll remind them." After I heard the front door close, I turned up the volume on the stereo so I could really enjoy it.

The twins and I had already decided we'd have to take plenty of food to last through our surveillance, so instead of going down to make my usual snack, I packed a lunch for later.

I was packing three sandwiches (in case the twins didn't bring sandwiches, and I had to share) into a bag, along with three Hershey bars and an apple, when Mark came in. He stared at the packed lunch.

"What's going on?"

"Cindy go to bed yet?"

"Yeah, she's reading in bed. What're you doing?"

"Packing a lunch," I said. "I wish Mom didn't have a rule about not eating the rest of the dessert. I'd like a piece of cake."

"What's going on?" he asked again.

I gave him a hard look. "Can you keep your mouth shut?"

"Sure. Hey, are you going over to the Hanson house? Are you? Can I go along?"

80

"No," I said.

"Why not?" His eyes were shining. "What're you going to do? Are you going to break in the house?"

"You think I want to go to jail? No, we're just going to watch and see if the guys stay there all night."

"All night? You're going to stay all night?"

"Well, maybe not, if they go away earlier."

"Who's going with you? The Swan twins?"

I decided to add granola bars—three of those, too, to be on the safe side. "I guess that's everything. They're supposed to have a Thermos of hot cocoa."

Mark eyed my sack. "I hope you don't have to run, carrying all that, plus a Thermos bottle. Listen, Steve, let me come! I won't get in your way, honest. And if anything happens, I'll run for help. Next door to Mrs. Constantine's."

"It won't come to that," I said. "We're just going to watch, that's all. Nobody's going to need help."

"You can't know that for sure. They're ugly guys, Steve. If they find out you're watching them, who knows what they'll do?"

"All the more reason for you to stay home," I told him. "Mom would kill me if I took you somewhere and you got hurt. Go up to bed and cover for me, if Dad looks in or anything."

He stared at me, disappointed. "How'll I do that?"

"I don't know. Think of something. Say I went out in the back yard to see why Sandy was barking."

"What if Sandy's not barking?"

"You know Dad. If he's watching TV he'll never know whether Sandy barks or not. Just don't tell him I've gone to the Hanson place, or away from home at all. Turn out the light and leave a tape in the machine; he'll think I'm listening to music. Turn it down low, so he won't come in and do it. OK?"

"I still wish you'd let me go," Mark agreed reluctantly.

"Well, I won't, so forget it. I'll tell you all about it tomorrow."

I picked up the sack and reached for my jacket. There was a prickle down my spine as I let myself out the back door into the darkness.

9

It wasn't a cold night. I wasn't sure if it was lucky there was no moon or not. I wouldn't have minded being able to see better, but on the other hand if we could see better, so could *they.*

Of course it wasn't *totally* dark. There was a streetlight on the corner. I got to the hedge at the front of the house first; the twins showed up a few minutes later, before I'd had time to start worrying.

Ray had his dad's big leather photographer's bag slung over his shoulder. He patted it. "Lunch," he said, grinning.

"You see anything yet?" Ray asked.

"Not a thing." I cleared my throat and then

wished I hadn't. I sounded nervous. "Let's go to the back then, OK?"

"We going in from the front or the back?" Ricky wanted to know. "The streetlight shines on this end of the sidewalk."

"You think we should go around and come in by the alley?" I asked. Suddenly it seemed like a good idea.

There were lights on in Mrs. Constantine's house, next door. "She'll hear it, if there's any racket," Ricky said.

"Why should there be any racket?" Ray asked. "We're just going to keep the place under surveillance, aren't we? Determine if those guys are living there, or if they go away at night."

Several dogs barked when we started down the alley. I knew most of them by name; when I spoke, quietly, they calmed down. Old Hercules even licked my fingers through the fence when we went past the Sarella place.

"You got some neat friends, Steve," Ricky said, and I thought he was smiling.

"Sure. If they'll just shut up so nobody investigates what we're doing out here," I muttered.

There wasn't much light in the alley. We were forced to turn on one of the flashlights after I ran into a garbage can and knocked the lid off. It made a heck of a noise. My heart was pounding like crazy by the time I got it put back on the can, and the dogs had stopped barking again.

I threw a beam of light ahead of us, then turned it off. "No more cans in the way. Let's go. We'll go under the hedge on Mrs. Constantine's side, right?"

We moved cautiously and quietly. My paper sack rustled. I wished I'd had a camera case or something quieter to carry my lunch in.

There was no light visible from the back of the Hanson house. We stood for a minute on the drive. "Maybe we ought to see if there's a car in the garage," I suggested. "See if they're home."

We eased up toward the garage. The door was closed, we could tell that in the little light that seeped through from the street. Ray tested it. "Locked," he said.

"There's a window around the side," I said. "I'll shine a light in there."

I did, holding my breath for fear somebody was in there, though it was absolutely silent. The garage was empty.

I flicked off the light again. "OK. Nobody here now. Let's establish ourselves over there, under the hedge. If we pick the place right by that fir tree, we can sit up in the open until somebody comes, and then slide back under the hedge."

The fir was tall and thick, with branches that nearly swept the ground. We put our stuff well under the hedge, then sat down to wait, hidden from anybody who'd drive in unless the headlights were aimed right at the fir tree.

We sat there for a few minutes without saying anything. I heard Ray squirming around. "The ground is wet," he said.

"Dew," Ricky informed him. "I'm getting hungry. Give me one of those baloney sandwiches, will you?"

I heard the rasp of the zipper as Ray got into the photographer's case. A minute later a Baggy was handed to me. I could smell the mustard.

After we'd each had a couple of cookies, we shared a cup of cocoa, steaming hot. Ray was about to pour us a second cup when we heard the car come into the alley. Its lights went out as it turned off the street.

I stiffened. Beside me, I heard Ray fumble, getting the cap on the Thermos bottle, cramming it into the leather case. "It's them," he whispered. "Who else would turn off their lights?"

It was the van, all right. It swung into the driveway a few feet beyond our sheltering tree. Though the headlights were out, the brake lights came on when it stopped; the red glow seemed eerie in the blackness, sort of like the eyes of those slimy monsters from the movie that had given Mark nightmares.

Somebody jumped out. We heard him with the key, and then the garage door went up; the van was driven inside.

I could hear Ricky breathing. I thought Ray was holding his breath, the same as I was.

All three of them were there. They left the garage door open; a light came on inside the van when they opened its rear door, and we all craned our necks to see through the fir boughs.

The fat one, Eddie, said, "I'll open the door. You guys carry the rest of it in, OK?"

"I'm glad this is the last of it." I didn't recognize that voice, so I decided it must be Harry. "I'm getting tired of working and only getting fed about half the time."

Skinny-with-the-watch, who I now knew was Cliff Hanson, reached into the van for one of the cartons. "Maybe we should have tried pizza. Maybe that crazy dog wouldn't like pizza." He swung around, facing us. He was silhouetted against the dome light in the van. "Just one thing, Harry. You make sure this stuff is out of here by the time my folks get back from Bermuda. My dad's putting the place on the market then, and I don't want any connection between me and this stuff."

"Relax," Harry said. He picked up a carton, too, and they started toward the house. "We'll be out of here in a month, just the way we agreed. You'll have your cut, and I'll go on to the next town. You gotta admit, it's a pretty easy way to earn money. And like I told you, if you want to come in with us when we leave town, we're willing to take in a third partner, permanently."

Their feet were noisy on the gravel as they all three moved toward the house, and I couldn't make out what they said after that. They went up the steps, a light came on in the kitchen.

Ricky flattened himself on the ground to look into the garage without having to stare through the fir branches. "What the heck do they have in those boxes?"

"One of us could sneak over there for a closer look," I said. "Maybe it says something on the cartons. Chances are they'll be inside for a minute or two."

"You volunteering to go?" Ray asked, just above a whisper. "Let's wait and see how long they stay inside, first. Hey, look! A light came on in the basement! See, there's a crack of light around the edge of the cardboard in that first window!"

There was, but although it indicated they'd gone into the cellar, or at least one of them had, it wasn't a big enough crack to see much through.

Nobody came out of the house. I began to wish I'd dashed over the minute they vanished inside and taken a look at the cartons, maybe even grabbed one. Now, with every moment that passed, the chances increased that we'd get caught if we tried anything like that.

"They're going to unload the whole van," Ricky murmured. "The next time they get a batch of boxes, one of us better try for a closer look."

"We going to draw straws?" Ray asked. I guessed by that that *he* didn't want to be the one to try it.

"I'll go," I said, "if I get a chance. Be ready to run, though, if anybody comes out of the house. If I have to run, I'm going down the alley, toward home."

"If we get separated," Ricky suggested, "we'll meet on the corner of Maple and Pine, OK?"

"Everybody go in a different direction," Ray said. "I'll run the opposite way in the alley from Steve. Ricky, you head for the front. That'll mean they have to split up to chase us. At least one of us will get away, more'n likely."

"What happens if somebody gets caught?" Ricky said. "Do the others call the cops?"

"We call the cops, and our folks are all going to know," Ray pointed out. "What do you think, Steve?"

"I think we're going to have to play it by ear. It'll depend on what they do. If they just chew one of us out, forget it. But if they try any rough stuff, we better call the police."

We all jerked backward when the door opened and Eddie came out. He sounded like an elephant coming down the steps.

Something brushed against my cheek, and I nearly screamed.

I threw myself sideways, and then realized what it was. Mrs. Constantine's black cat, Toby. I was starting to relax when Eddie stopped and spoke to the two men who'd come out of the house behind him.

"You guys hear anything?"

"No, what?"

"Over there, by that tree. I thought I heard something." Eddie was looking straight at us, and even though I knew he couldn't possibly see us, I broke out in a cold sweat.

"Wouldn't be that old lady again, not this time of night," Harry said.

90

"Mrs. Constantine," Cliff said. "She's a nosy old biddy, calls in the law whenever somebody's dog goes on her lawn or some kid trips over her hose. I told you before we started, we'd have to be careful about her."

"Eddie talked to her. She thinks we're cleaning the place up before it goes on sale. With that hedge between this house and hers, she's not going to see anything at night, not as careful as we're being," Harry said.

"Well, she better not see me," Cliff said. "I don't want her telling my old man I was monkeying around here while he was gone."

"Don't sweat it, man," Harry said. "Hey, I thought I heard something, too."

The confounded cat had walked past Ray, tail switching right under Ray's nose. Ray's allergic to cats. He made a terrific effort to stop the sneeze, so it came out a sort of strangled snort.

"Maybe we better take a look," Eddie said. "Where'd you leave the flashlight?"

"On the front seat of the van."

Beside me I heard Ray contorting in an effort to smother a second sneeze. I knew I had to do something, and fast.

Sorry, Toby, I thought, and grabbed for the cat. I raised up, hoping I was invisible against the hedge, and threw Toby out onto the driveway.

Toby was bewildered and angry. He spat and ran, past the open door of the garage, into the alley. A minute later we heard a dog bark once.

Harry laughed. "A cat. Nothing but a cat."

"A black cat," Cliff said. "Black cats are bad luck."

"Baloney," Harry told him, turning toward the garage. "We make our own luck. Just keep your mind on the money at the end of the month, Cliff. Come on, let's get the rest of this unloaded."

We sat there for nearly half an hour while they carried in carton after carton. The boxes didn't seem terribly heavy, but there were a lot of them. Apparently they were putting them in the basement; that crack of light stayed there, around the edge of one of the pieces of cardboard. Finally when they were all three inside, I took a deep breath.

"I'm going to try to see inside," I said and, keeping low, dashed across the driveway to the basement window. My feet sounded like rocks on a tin roof; I thought sure somebody would hear me. They wouldn't think *that* was a cat.

It was a wasted effort. All I could see through the narrow slit was a bit of concrete block wall and a section of furnace pipe secured to the ceiling. No boxes, no people.

"Steve! Freeze!"

The hissed command made me freeze, all right. I dropped to the ground, close to the house, heart pounding and feeling clammy all over.

I heard them coming out the back door; I eased slowly backward, cut off from the twins; if they spotted me now I would have to run around the other side of the house and hope I got through to the street. From the way these guys had talked, I was sure they wouldn't just let me go if they caught me.

I crouched on the damp earth, trembling, trying to control my breathing so it wouldn't give me away.

They had loaded up with cartons again. Their voices were low, but they were talking as if they thought they were alone. "One more load," Harry said. "When we're done, let's lock up and go eat. Chinese food, maybe. That China Jade place stay open this late?"

"It's open until midnight," Cliff said. "Yeah, I'll go for that. I don't know what's the matter, something's spooking me tonight. I'll be glad when this is over."

"Your part almost is, buddy. Eddie's taking care of sales. All you have to do now is put the keys back after everything's been delivered, before your daddy gets home. For a guy who was brave enough to dip into his own old man's till, and then 'borrow' from the cash box at a gas station, you sure are chicken-livered, Cliff."

"Stupid," Eddie said, holding a carton against his middle, "to swipe money at the gas station, when you was the only one there. Why didn't you say you was robbed or something?"

They disappeared inside again. I couldn't see the door or the kitchen lights, so I waited until I heard Ricky's loud whisper. "Now, Steve!"

I felt as if somebody was going to shoot me in the back as I made a dash for the fir tree.

"You see anything?" Ray asked.

"No. Nothing."

The van was finally empty. They came out in less time than before, got in the van, and backed it out of the garage. Cliff relocked the door, and they drove away, still without lights.

We sat there in silence for a minute or two. "Now what?" I asked.

"We have to find out what's in those boxes," Ricky said. "Come on, they're gone; they won't be back tonight. Let's take the flashlights and look around, see if there's a door or a window unlocked or something."

It was a relief to stand up.

"We're not going to break in, are we?" Ray asked.

"No, but if there's a way in—not *breaking* in—I'd feel justified in looking around in there," I said. I felt braver now that they'd gone. "If we knew what was in the boxes, we could call the police."

We left our lunches under the fir tree and, with both flashlights on, headed toward the house.

10

We went all around the house, checking every door and every window. They were securely locked. We shined our lights through the ground floor windows—the basement ones were blocked by the cardboard—and saw nothing but empty rooms.

Finally, frustrated and tired, we got our stuff from under the hedge and sat on the edge of the porch to eat the last of it.

"This was all for nothing," Ray said.

"No, it wasn't," I told him. "We know they're only here to store their boxes, whatever they have in them, and this was the last they'll bring in. Eddie's supposed to be taking care of sales. He'll have to come here to get the merchandise. They're keeping a low profile, trying not to make the neighbors suspicious, and they don't know we're onto them. It's for sure illegal, whatever they're doing. We've got a couple of weeks to catch them and turn them over to the police. That's not a waste of time."

"How're we going to find out the rest of what we need to know?" Ray asked.

None of us knew the answer to that one. "Maybe we'll have to keep on staking the place out," Ricky said wearily, stretching. "Come on, let's go get some sleep. We'll think about it, and come up with something."

I sure didn't think of anything clever to do, not that wasn't illegal, too. I typed up my list of new customers for the *Times* on Mom's portable on Saturday, hoping that before I had to turn it in on Monday afternoon I'd have a few more subscriptions from the staff at school. I wracked my brain to think of anybody else I could contact.

I could have gone outside my territory, on the fringes of it, anyway, but I knew what my dad would say about that. I'd heard it several times before.

"I never understood how anybody gets any satisfaction out of 'winning' if he has to cheat to do it," he'd say.

Once I'd come back with something like, "Well, whoever wins gets the prize. I suppose that's satisfaction enough for some people, to have the prize."

"It wouldn't be to me," Dad said. "I'd feel as if I'd stolen it if I didn't get it fair and square."

I guessed that was the way it hit me, too. But my list of new subscribers didn't seem very impressive, not when I remembered the expression on Shorty Bergen's face when he'd informed me it was going to be his name at the top of the prize list on Wednesday. It was depressing.

To console myself, I wandered over to Rotten Ralphie's and perched on a stool until he came over and rested his hands on the counter. "Hi, Steve. You look glum. How can I cheer you up?"

"With a Jumbo burger. And onion rings." I *was* depressed, I needed something special. I hardly ever treated myself to onion rings. "And a chocolate shake." I was really splurging, but I didn't care. If my name wasn't at the top of that prize list on Wednesday, maybe I'd come back and have the same again.

"Coming up," Ralphie said. He slapped hamburger patties on the griddle and reached for the buns.

I stared at his broad white back. "I don't suppose

you'd like a subscription to the *Times,* would you, Ralphie?"

I knew that was the wrong way to solicit business. You *never* approach a prospective customer in a negative way, Dad says. Always act as if you expect them to say yes. I didn't expect Ralphie to say yes, so what difference did it make?

He turned around, holding a spatula in one hand. "Already take it at home. Shorty Bergen delivers it. My doggone kids have it all torn to shreds by the time I get home; first thing I do, when I walk in the door, is gather up the sections— the sports section is always missing—and put it together so I can read it. Sorry, Steve."

I perked up. "Hey, you know what you should do?"

"No, what?"

"You should have a second subscription here. I know you have times when you can sit down for a while, when there're no customers. If you had a paper delivered here in the morning, you could read it during the slow times, no looking for the sports section."

He looked at me, pursing his lips. "You're some salesman, aren't you?"

"I have several customers who take two copies," I told him. "For similar reasons. They have time to read on their jobs during the day, and they don't like reading a paper that's been taken apart or their wife's cut recipes or sale ads out of."

Ralphie flipped the hamburger patties and looked at me again. "My wife does cut out recipes," he said thoughtfully. "I asked her why she couldn't wait until I'd read the paper, and she said she'd forget and I'd burn the papers before she remembered."

"I could drop a paper off on my way to school," I said.

Suddenly he laughed. "OK, you made a sale. Sign me up."

So that was one more to add to my list. I wished I knew how many Shorty Bergen had on *his*.

I felt better after one of Ralphie's Jumbo burgers. I decided to treat myself to another tape, too.

I walked on over to Henry's Electronics, pausing to see if the sign for the half-price sale was still in the window. It was. I pushed open the door and went in.

Henry—I supposed he was Henry, he was the only one I'd seen in there—waved a hand from behind the counter. "Come back for some tapes, young man?"

"Well, one, maybe."

"Two for the price of one, the prices everybody else charges," he said. "Have two, son."

I went over to the bin to look at them. They weren't arranged in any kind of order, so you had to pick them up, one by one, and look at them to tell what he had.

I couldn't make up my mind between a new tape by Georgia and the Peach Fuzz and an old one by Willie's Billies. I had one in each hand when Henry wandered over and grinned at me. "Want 'em both? You'll never beat the price."

"Yeah, I know." I sighed. "OK, I'll take both of them."

"You're getting a bargain," he told me, slipping them in a sack. "Tell your friends, kid. While they last. When they're gone, it'll be regular prices again."

"You get a special deal on them?" I asked.

"That's right. I get a bargain, my customers get a bargain."

I turned away toward the front door and suddenly changed my mind about going that way. Shorty Bergen was crossing the street, coming straight toward me. "Uh, is it OK if I go out the back door? Into the alley?" I asked.

"Sure, why not? Straight through the storeroom,

101

there. Just be sure to latch the door. I don't want just anybody wandering in that way, not when I'm here alone," he said.

I went through a crowded storage area, with boxes piled high on both sides of a narrow aisle, and into the alley. I was glad I didn't have to talk to Shorty again. I was tired of the way he kept telling me he was going to win the contest.

I was thinking about that instead of looking where I was going, so I'd walked through a puddle of motor oil in the alley before I realized it was there. I left tracks like the pattern on the soles of my running shoes for about thirty yards. I couldn't believe how many people drove cars that leaked oil that way.

Nothing much happened the rest of the weekend. On Sunday we went to my cousin Laurie's wedding. We had to get all dressed up, which was a pain, but the food was good. Mark ate so much he got sick.

I hurried through deliveries on Monday morning. I left a paper at Ralphie's—he was busy with the breakfast crowd and just waved a hand at me— and then got to school as fast as I could so I could distribute the free papers. I left one each with Mr. Biteman, with Mrs. Peters, and with Mr. Jacobsmeyer. I told each of them I'd appreciate knowing at the end of the school day if they were interested in signing up for a regular subscription, because it was the last day of the contest.

I could tell when I got into the line at the cafeteria behind Ricky that he was excited about something.

"What's up?" I asked.

"I had an idea," Ricky said, reaching for a plate of mashed potatoes and gravy and a hot dog.

"A dumb idea," Ray said, from ahead of him in the line.

"Yeah? What?"

"Tell you in private," Ricky said, grinning. He added a piece of cake to his tray. "I'll save a seat."

I picked up my own lunch and followed the twins to a table. "What's your idea?" I demanded.

Ricky looked around to see if anybody was paying any attention to us. The cafeteria was always like a zoo. We wouldn't have attracted attention if we'd each had two heads.

"I figured out how we can get into the Hanson house."

"Yeah?" I forgot about eating and leaned forward. "How?"

"It's stupid," Ray said. "We'll get caught for sure."

"How?" I demanded.

"Well, we don't have keys, right? And we're not

going to do anything so they can charge us with breaking and entering, right? So when's the only time the doors are unlocked?"

I stared at him. "When those guys are there, carrying stuff in or out."

"Right. So *that's* when we go in."

"You're crazy," I told him.

"That's what I said. He's crazy," Ray echoed.

"You want to get us killed, or what?" I asked.

"Arrested, at the very least," Ray said.

Ricky gave his brother an exasperated look. "We're not planning to get caught, stupid. The whole point is just to get inside the house and see what's in the boxes."

"You must have given this some thought," I answered. "Explain to me how this is going to work."

Ray scowled at me. "Now you're both crazy."

"It won't hurt to listen," I said.

"Right!" Ricky began to eat, talking between bites. "It's a big house, and it's empty, except for those boxes in the cellar. If one of us could slip in while they're all down there, and the door is standing open, he could hide anywhere else. They'd have no reason to suspect that anybody was in the house, would they? One of us could go inside, go up the stairs until they're gone, and then come down and open the front door from inside for the other two of us."

"One of us!" Ray made a snorting sound. "Not *me*. Don't expect *me* to do anything so stupid."

Ricky ignored him. "I looked at that front door lock the other night. It's the kind that locks with a button on the inside, so once we had someone in the house, we could use that door."

"Chances are," Ray said, "we'd end up in jail."

"It'd be risky," I said. "I mean, they don't all three necessarily go down in the basement at the same time."

"They might, though. If they did, it would be easy enough to slip in and get into another room. The door to the basement is in the kitchen, so all you'd have to do is get across that one lighted room and wait until they left."

"Who's this *you* you keep talking about?" Ray asked.

Ricky ignored that, too. By this time, I was sufficiently intrigued to add my own two cents worth.

"It might work. If they didn't all go downstairs at the same time, maybe we could create a diversion that would draw them to the same place and let one of us get inside."

"Sure," Ray said. "We could burn down the garage, and they'd all go tearing out there, and the fire trucks would come, and we'd be arrested for arson."

Ricky punched him lightly on the arm. "Shut up. Steve's right. A diversion might work even better than my original idea. No fires, nothing dangerous. Or I know! Your dog, Steve. That goofy Sandy."

"Sandy?" I wasn't sure I liked the sound of involving Sandy. "He's not exactly predictable," I said.

"It's predictable he'll go after the smell of hamburger. Or anything else that smells like food. If we could make it look as if Sandy ran into the house, nobody—not even the police—would blame us for chasing him and getting him out, would they? Even the thieves wouldn't know that we were onto *them;* they'd just be annoyed with us." Ricky was struck by another brilliant idea. "If we chased Sandy inside, we could unlock the front door—all you have to do is twist the button—and come back later, after the guys have gone."

I considered that while Ricky waited with a hopeful look.

"It has possibilities," I said finally.

Ray shook his head. "I wonder if they'll let me come visit both of you in jail," he said.

11

I thought about Ricky's idea so much I got bawled out in two different classes that afternoon for day-dreaming. I imagined everything that could happen; I was still leery of involving Sandy because he probably wouldn't do what we wanted him to do, and I wouldn't want anything to happen to him.

I was thinking about it so hard I almost forgot to check back and see if I'd made any newspaper subscription sales. I had. All three of them.

I thanked them profusely and added their names to my list, then walked down to the *Times* office and turned it in.

Mr. Walker, the circulation manager, looked at

my list. "You're going for the big one, are you, Steve?"

"Sure. Has Shorty Bergen turned his list in yet?"

"Ten minutes ago," Mr. Walker said. "You and Shorty are the best we've got. You always get out there and work."

"Who's got the most? Shorty or me?"

He laughed and shook his head. "You know better than that. Read the name of the winner in Wednesday's paper."

Tuesday Ricky and I talked about our plan every time we got together—in the cafeteria, at P.E. until the coach yelled at us to get back on the field, during study hall by way of notes passed back and forth, and after school. We decided we would have Sandy on hand to create the diversion only if the guys didn't all go into the basement at once. Then the question was when to do it. We didn't know if the guys came most often in the daytime or at night; so we set up a schedule so that one or the other of us would walk past the house regularly, and let the others know when they showed up.

Even Ray agreed to patrol. He just kept saying he wasn't going to get involved in anything dangerous or stupid.

It was still dark Wednesday morning when I

picked up my papers. I wondered if Shorty had his yet. It was too dark to read, but I had a headlight on my bike.

It was awkward, trying to open up a newspaper and find the contest results on an inner page, with only the headlight from a bicycle. I finally found it, page four of Section C.

"First Prize," it said, "winner of the portable radio-tape-player, STEVE QUENTIN."

I let out a whoop that made the dogs start barking across the street.

"Second Prize," it said, "winner of his choice of four free tapes from Smitty's Video and Electronics, Clarence Bergen."

I felt great. I could hardly wait to get my papers delivered, get home and tell Mom. "I'll be late after school. I have to go down to the *Times* office to pick up my prize," I said.

The Swan twins were waiting for me when I got to their house on the way to school. "Guess what?" Ricky greeted me.

"What?"

"Mom had a meeting last night, so Dad took us to Rotten Ralphie's for supper. We sat in one of the booths, and guess who was in the one next to us?"

"Cliff and Eddie and Harry?"

"Right! They didn't pay any attention to us, but we listened to *them*."

"What did they say?"

"They said," Ricky announced triumphantly, "that they had a shipment to get out—tonight! They're going to meet there at nine. Be just about dark then. Cliff's going to help because Harry broke his hand and can't carry the boxes. He's in a cast."

"Sounded like he got in a fight with somebody," Ray offered.

"Tonight," I echoed, feeling that knot forming in my stomach again. "Are we going to go for it? Be there when they get there?"

"I vote yes," Ricky said.

"I do, too," I said.

We both looked at Ray. Finally he shrugged. "I guess so. It wouldn't be any fun being out of jail all by myself."

That night I got Mark aside as soon as we'd finished supper.

"You still want in on the big operation?" I asked him.

He brightened. "Yeah, sure. What's going to happen?"

I told him what we were planning to do. "The

diversion is going to be Sandy. You can come along if you'll hold him, and *keep him quiet,* until we see if we need him. If we do, I'll throw a hamburger through the door, and all you have to do is wait outside while we get him out. If we don't come out right away, or if they catch us and cause trouble, you run for Mrs. Constantine's and tell her to call the police."

His eyes sparkled. "OK! When do we go?"

It wasn't completely dark when we got there. Sandy smelled the hamburgers, all right; it was a hard job keeping him away from the sack, which I'd tucked inside my jacket.

We hid behind the big fir again, though since it wasn't as dark as before we weren't sure we were safely hidden.

"Hey," Ray said almost as soon as we were settled, "here they come. No lights again, so Mrs. Constantine won't notice them."

Sandy whined, and Mark squatted beside him, stroking him, soothing him. "Keep him quiet," I hissed, and then it was too late to talk any more. They were turning in the driveway.

They didn't bother with the garage this time; they backed the van as close as they could to the rear steps, and got out. We could see the white of the cast on Harry's wrist. "Let's go, move it out," Harry said.

He went around and opened the rear doors, so that light spilled out of the van onto the back steps. Cliff opened the house door and turned on the kitchen light, just as expected.

As soon as the men disappeared inside, Ray moved out, keeping close to the hedge. He'd brought his dad's binoculars and a little pen flashlight.

There was an old apple tree in the side yard. We'd looked at it in daylight and decided that if Ray climbed to a low branch, he'd be able to look into the kitchen and signal when was a good time to run for it.

"He made it that far," Ricky muttered, when the little pen light blinked at us. It had red cellophane over the lens.

"Watch for the signal," Ricky said, close to my ear. We'd already drawn straws, and I'd won—or was it lost? Anyway, I was the one who was going to sprint for the house when Ray signaled that the kitchen was clear.

It came. A winking red pinpoint in the darkness. On, off, on, off.

My heart was in my throat, my stomach a tight knot.

"Go!" Ricky whispered.

I sprinted across the grass, hitting the edge of the gravel, then up the steps more slowly, being as quiet as I could. I took a deep breath and stepped inside the lighted kitchen, feeling as if I were meeting a firing squad.

It was empty, just the way it was supposed to be. I hesitated. The door was open to the basement, and the light had been turned on down there. And then I froze, for I heard voices from one of the dark, unfurnished rooms off the kitchen.

That wasn't part of the scenario we'd imagined, and I panicked. They were where I was supposed to go!

"Here, this is what I've collected so far," Eddie's voice said. "Comes to six hundred and eighty dollars apiece. That enough to calm your jitters, Cliff?"

It was either the basement, or back out the door I'd just entered. I didn't have time to think. I practically dived down the cellar stairs.

"You hear something?" Harry asked, above and behind me.

"You forget to shut the door? One of those confounded dogs will be getting in again," Cliff said.

What happened next wasn't quite the way we'd planned, either. I didn't know for sure what was happening at first, because I heard running feet and scratching on the kitchen linoleum, followed by barking and yelling.

"Catch him!"

"Get him out of here!"

"Shut the door!"

"Hey, who're you?"

"My dog!" Ricky said, his voice going up in a squeak. "My dog ran in here!"

Somebody slammed the door at the top of the stairs. I looked around at a big room full of cardboard cartons and took another dive behind a row of them that stood out from the wall. As I stood there—breathing heavily, wondering what was going on upstairs and what I was going to do if they caught me down there—I smelled hamburger and onions.

For a minute I was confused. Then I realized what I'd done. I'd forgotten about the hamburgers when Ray gave the signal; I was still carrying them inside my jacket.

After that it wasn't hard to figure out what had happened. Sandy had seen his long-smelled lunch disappearing, and he'd gone after it. It was lucky he hadn't pursued me down here before someone got the door closed.

I heard him barking now, and Ricky's raised voice. "I'm sorry, I don't know what's the matter with him. He jumps in cars or goes in houses when the doors are left open. I'll get him out of here!"

"You do that," Eddie said in a menacing way, and then they must have all moved out onto the porch. Though I continued to hear voices, I couldn't make out the words any more.

Nobody was coming down here, at least not yet. I looked at the nearest stack of boxes. They didn't have any labels on them, and I decided to do what I'd come for. Find out what was in them.

I ripped up the sealed flaps and stared into the box.

Tapes? Cassette tapes? It didn't make any sense. Or did it?

Wally and the Nuts, a whole carton of them. I'd seen some just like this in the bin at Henry's Electronics.

And all of a sudden it *did* make sense. It was as if I'd been putting together pieces of a puzzle for days, without being able to tell what the picture was going to be.

Now I knew.

Tapes. Tapes being sold at "the lowest prices in town" at Henry's, half what Smitty had to charge for them. I'd even seen Eddie at Henry's, and there had been all that leaked oil outside Henry's back door...just like the oil that had dripped out on the gravel here behind the house. And cartons in Henry's back room, just like these. I opened another box and found the same thing.

The door opened above and heavy feet sounded on the stairs. I crouched low and crept farther along between the boxes and the wall.

"Stupid kids," Eddie said. "It's the same dog that kept swiping our lunches. I must be losing my mind. I can smell hamburgers and onions right now."

"I don't like it," Cliff said. "I don't like it that the neighborhood kids saw us here. Some of them might recognize me later if any of this comes out."

They were just on the other side of the stack of cartons, so close I felt they were breathing on me. I held my breath, but there wasn't anything I could do about the way my heart was hammering.

"Don't be a fool," Eddie said. "The kids didn't see anything."

"They saw me!" Cliff said angrily. "I wasn't supposed to be in on this part of it at all, but Harry had to go and break his wrist—"

"I didn't do it on purpose," Harry said, sounding just as angry. "Stop talking about moving stuff; we aren't moving anything. Come on. Henry's going to have the back door open for us in an hour, and we're wasting time. After we unload at his place, we still have to run the rest of the load over to Martinville. Let's go."

They went clomping back upstairs, laden with cartons. Harry wasn't carrying any because of his cast, and I was afraid he'd stay down there, but he didn't.

As soon as they reached the main floor, I started up the stairs after them. My stupid heart was making so much noise I doubted that I'd hear them if they were stopped in the kitchen, but I had to get out of there as fast as I could.

I found out afterward that Mark and Ricky had recaptured Sandy and pulled him back to our earlier hiding place, where they were joined by Ray when he left the apple tree. They didn't know for sure where I'd gone, or why the men hadn't seen me; they were waiting for me to reappear or the other guys to leave.

If they'd just had Mark take Sandy and go on home with him, it would have been all right. It didn't occur to any of them, though, and the minute I showed up in that lighted doorway, it was pure pandemonium.

Sandy saw me and remembered I was the one who had the hamburgers. He started barking furiously and jerked free from Mark, who wasn't prepared for anything like that lunge.

The men had put their cartons in the back of the van and were returning for more.

Everybody yelled, and Sandy barked. He reached me first, jumping up on me, yapping with joy that he'd almost attained the hamburgers.

"Run, Steve!" the kids were shouting, only there wasn't much choice of where to run to, with any chance of getting away.

We'd agreed to split up if anything like this happened. Mark was so paralyzed he just stood there; if Ray hadn't grabbed his arm and dragged him away, he'd have been caught in seconds.

And catching us was what they had in mind.

"Don't let them get away!" Cliff was yelling, and he dashed after Mark and Ray.

Sandy did me one favor. He was excited, and when I managed to get the sack from Rotten Ralphie's out of my jacket and give it a fling, he dived for it, tripping Harry as he came up onto the porch. I vaulted over the railing between Harry and Eddie. Eddie reached for me just as Ricky swung his dad's binoculars by the leather strap and clipped him alongside the head with them.

Eddie was more surprised than hurt, but it took him off guard enough so I dived past him. "Run," Ricky said unnecessarily, and we pelted toward the alley.

We made a lot of racket. I caught a glimpse of lights coming on through the hedge at Mrs. Constantine's, but there wasn't time to wait for her to call the police. These guys were going to murder us before the cops could get there.

I heard their pounding feet behind us—Eddie and Harry both, I guessed—and knew we weren't going to outrun them. I grabbed out at Ricky, panting so hard I didn't know if I could say it. "Follow me! Over the Sarellas' fence!"

We rolled over it and hit the ground, hard. I heard *their* feet behind us, harder yet.

"Hey," Ricky gasped, staggering into me, "this is where—"

If he finished that, I didn't hear him. What I heard was Hercules.

I couldn't see him, I could only imagine that big black Doberman head, those gleaming yellow eyes and the teeth like a saber-toothed tiger. "Hercules!" I yelled, so he'd know it was me. "Go get 'em, boy!"

Ricky and I fell against the side of the Sarella garage, and Hercules went right on past us. I felt the air moving, then heard the grunt as Hercules took one of them down.

He was snarling, barking, and they screamed. Even if we did want Hercules to save us, it was sort of horrible to hear.

A light came on at the rear of the house, and Mr. Sarella ran out. "What's going on?"

"Thieves, robbers," I said, though that wasn't really what I intended to say. "Call the police!"

"That you, Steve? What's going on? Sounds like the police are already coming." We all heard the siren as Mr. Sarella advanced into the yard. "Down, Hercules! Down, boy!"

Hercules minded Mr. Sarella better than he'd minded me. He sank onto his haunches now, visible in the yardlight, tongue lolling between those wicked teeth, still growling. When the light came on, Harry vaulted back into the alley and took off, but Hercules had Eddie cornered between the fence and the garbage cans. The fat man was holding up his hands in front of him. "Call him off! Get him away from me! He's chewed my leg half off!"

120

"He'll chew it the rest of the way off," Mr. Sarella said, "if you don't stand still."

Eddie stood still. We heard the siren and saw the flashing lights from the police cruiser when it drew up in the alley. Harry had chosen the wrong way to run; he was right in their headlights when they stopped and he had nowhere to go. At least not after an officer got out and yelled at him to hold it, right there. Harry lifted his hands in the air.

It got kind of confused after that. There were two police cars—it turned out Mrs. Sarella had called as well as Mrs. Constantine, so the police figured there really was something going on—and half the neighborhood came out to see.

The cop who took charge wanted to know what had happened, so we told him. Ray and Mark came back after they saw the police cars. Cliff had actually had a hand on Mark's arm, but he bolted and ran when he heard the sirens. We all talked at once until the officer lifted a hand to shut us up.

"Hold it, hold it! You," he said, stabbing a pen in my direction, "tell me what happened."

It took me a while. Mr. and Mrs. Sarella and Mrs. Constantine and half my paper route customers stood around and listened.

121

When I got to the part about opening one of the cartons, Ricky asked eagerly, "What was in them, Steve?"

"Tapes. Cassette tapes."

"Tapes?" several people echoed. The cop stopped making notes. "Tapes?" he said. "Musical tapes?"

"Yeah. I figured it out, I think. They're pirated. I mean, they've duplicated them, illegally, and that's why they can sell them cheaper to the dealers, and why Henry's Electronics can sell them at half price. They don't pay the original artists anything for them; they steal from them. It's illegal to pirate somebody else's music, isn't it?"

"Sure is," the officer agreed. "Come on, fella," he said to Eddie, "get in the back of the squad car with your friend. What's the name of the one you say got away?"

We told him. He said they'd want us to go down to headquarters tomorrow and answer some more questions, but we could all go home now.

Boy, that was some evening.

My dad was furious. He grounded me for two weeks. He would have made it longer except that everybody in town thought the four of us kids were heroes. He said he thought he was raising smarter kids than us, and that I deserved a lesson, especially for involving my little brother.

Mr. Swan was mad, too, even though his binoculars weren't damaged. He said it was no thanks to the twins, and they were grounded, too.

The story was on page three of the *Times*, and on the front page of the *Herald*. They didn't use our pictures, though. And nobody gave us a reward. Mostly the grownups chewed us out and told us never to get involved in anything like that again.

Ralphie thought it was exciting. When we told him we didn't get any reward or anything, he gave us all free Jumbos, with onion rings. He said he was glad we weren't any of us *his* kids.

I really appreciated my new tape-player. It kept me company while I made my paper deliveries. Since I wasn't allowed to go anywhere else, or do anything, for two weeks, it was the only entertainment I had.

The first day after we weren't grounded anymore, I saw something funny on the way home from school. I started to tell the family about it at supper. "There's something peculiar going on over at Montgomery's," I said. "There's this old lady, and she—"

My dad held up his hand. "Stop. Stop right there. Whatever is going on is none of your business.

Stay out of it, Steve. You understand? No more monsters in the closet or pirated tapes or anything else, and I mean it."

There was a small silence, and then Cindy said, "Can I tell about the story I wrote for school? I got an A on it."

"Of course, honey," Mom said. "What was it about?"

Cindy slid a glance in my direction. "Well, Steve made up the *first* one, but *I* made a story about it. It's about the purplish bloodsucker that lived under this little boy's bed, and one day he—"

Dad made a strangled sound. He looked at my mother.

"Good grief, we've got another one of them."

Mom started to laugh. "It looks that way. Quiet, everybody, let Cindy tell her story."

She did, and even Dad had to admit it, she had a lot of imagination.